VOODOO CHILD

VOODOO CHILD

B

The rights of Andre Duza and Wayne Simmons to be
identified as the authors of this work has been asserted
by them in accordance with the Copyright, Designs and
Patents Act 1988.

This is a work of fiction. All of the characters,
organisations and events portrayed in this novel are
either products of the authors' imaginations or are used
fictitiously.

First published in 2015 by Infected Books

A CIP catalogue record for this book
is available from the British Library

ISBN 978-0-9576563-5-2

www.infectedbooks.co.uk
@infectedbks

Cover illustration by Alex McVey
Cover design by Andre Duza
Edited by Brenda Wilkinson

www.houseofduza.com

www.waynesimmons.org

PROLOGUE

The knife was stained red. The blood dripped from its blade like thick sauce but still the girl held it, clammy hands clinging to the plastic grip like her life depended upon it.

And it did.

Her attacker stood in front of her. One hand covered the wound on his arm. The other was poised to strike.

He lunged but the girl managed to side step him, fleeing the kitchen with the knife still in her hands. She made for the front door to the apartment, pulling it open, but he was on her again before she could get through, pinning her against the door, face first.

She forced her head backwards, connecting with his nose.

He howled in pain, releasing his grip.

The girl pulled away, darting down the hallway and grabbing the cordless phone. She tried to type 911 but he was on her again. She ducked into the bedroom, but he grabbed her arm, making her drop the phone. She swung the knife in his direction. It found its target and he let go, stumbling backwards.

The girl slammed the bedroom door, fell back against it. Her eyes found the bathroom and she made for it, locking its door behind her and falling back onto the toilet seat.

Her breathing came heavy. Sweat broke across her brow.

Jesus, he's going to kill me. He's going to break through this door and kill me.

The phone was on the bedroom floor. She could hear it beeping, its dead tone almost deafening.

Please hang up. Please hang up.

Minutes passed. Maybe half an hour and still the girl sat there. Waiting. Breathing. Heart beating like a drum. The cordless had stopped wailing, its battery dead.

Maybe she'd got him good. Maybe she'd wounded him, slowed him down.

Maybe she'd killed him.

Slowly, the girl got up from the toilet, reached for the lock with one shaking hand. She pushed the door ajar, peered into the bedroom. The bedroom door was open but there was no sign of him.

She moved quickly towards the bedroom window. Peered down at a seven storey drop, thought about jumping. Instead, her eyes found the bedroom doorway and she started towards it, careful to make as little noise as possible.

A shift in the corner, something moving.

She swung around quickly, pointing the blade towards the movement. But it was nothing, just the curtain distracted by the wind.

A door creaking. She turned again, this time looking back towards the bathroom.

Nothing there.

The wardrobe caught her eye. It was old, like something from a fairy tale. There was blood on its doorknob but it wasn't her blood.

Maybe it's his blood...

She curled one trembling hand around the wardrobe's doorknob. Wrenched the door open, stabbing the hanging clothes inside uselessly with the blade.

She closed the wardrobe door, ran a hand through her hair.

Heavy breathing from behind.

The girl turned and he was on her again, this time reaching for the knife. But she was quick, falling back against the wardrobe and swiping the blade wildly across his eyes.

He screamed, face buried in his hands, blood seeping through the fingers.

She swung the knife again.

ONE

The opening riff to *Voodoo Child* played on the car stereo. Lori whooped in delight, patting the steering wheel in time with the music.

'Jesus, turn it down,' Roxy complained from the back.

'No, turn it *up*, baby!' Lori roared, reaching for the stereo volume and knocking the volume up a notch or two.

Roxy leaned back in her seat, folding her arms and pouting. 'It's 1985 for Christ's sake. You can't be playing that hippy shit no more. Haven't you got anything decent? Like *Motley Crue*?'

Lori just sang harder, goading Roxy in the mirror.

Abby smiled, shaking her head. It had been like this the whole journey.

She peered out the window, squinting against the sun. They passed signs for the 'new'

Black Water Campgrounds; some quick-hand-ed painting featuring all the usual activities (canoeing, paddle-boating, swimming, volley-ball, arcade) hosted by a cartoon grizzly who bore a striking resemblance to Yogi Bear, only the Black Water bear chomped on a cigar. 'They call him Stogie,' Lori told them, laughing, and then made some quip about commercializa-tion that Abby didn't quite get.

Abby's eyes found a lake, tucked between two patches of thick, dense woods. It looked like the kind of place they would say devil wor-shippers use, a place all the local kids would tell ghost stories about. Today it was packed with families and empty nesters. Still, the lake spooked her for some reason and Abby looked away.

It wasn't that she hated the water. She loved it. When she was a kid, her pop used to take her out hiking on the weekends. It was their little secret. Abby would tell her mom they were go-ing to some game or taking in a movie, instead heading to the woods, walking until they found some spring or other and then filling their bot-tles from the crystal clear water and drinking deeply.

She remembered her pop's car, one of those big off-road things with four-wheel drive and tires like rubber dinghies. Its trunk would be jam-packed with maps and hats and guns, Abby safe in the knowledge that her old man was prepared for just about anything on their trip.

Lori's car was the complete opposite. A tiny little Beetle, it wheezed its way along the road, music and smoke pouring from its rusty old hide. Lori claimed it ran on vegetable oil. Abby wasn't sure if that was true, but the Volkswagen looked the type with its curious dress of racing stripes and flower petals spray-painted across the bonnet.

It suited her friend to a T. Lori was every bit as maverick as her little car. The only child to a black mother and redneck father, she was probably the most beautiful looking girl Abby had ever laid eyes upon. She was also the only person Abby knew who called *herself* a witch.

'You'll love this place,' Lori said, one bangled hand in the air. 'The trees, the plains, the clean air, the water... It's kinda what I imagine Heaven to be like.'

'Oh here we go,' muttered Roxy. 'More of Lori's mystical BS.'

'Shut it,' Lori chided. 'Or I'll put my *Paul Simon* cassette in that stereo, and then you'll be sorry!'

Roxy laughed. 'Don't you fucking dare!'

Roxy was the kind of girl mothers feared, Abby thought. All heels and skirt and glam and boobs. Truth be told, Abby didn't really know her that well. She was more Lori's friend. But she had a rep around town, known for being a bit of a groupie type. Hell, she'd even slept with Danny.

No, don't go there.

'Still thinking about him?' Lori asked as if reading her mind

'No,' Abby lied. 'I told you, this trip is about getting away from all that. Spend time with my friends, be at one with Mother Nature.'

'The rebirth of Abby,' Lori mused. 'I like it. In fact, let's make that the theme of the whole weekend, yeah?'

Abby smiled, adjusted her glasses; a pair of round wireframes that, according to Lori, gave her a 'sexy librarian' look. Abby thought they made her look mousy. Although she was glad to get away, and moved by the effort it took to work around everybody's schedules, Abby was embarrassed by all the fuss being made over her.

Lori winked. 'Oh, and speaking of Mother Nature, I've got some of her finest right here, girl.' She patted the front pocket of her Daisy Dukes. 'Home grown Mary Jane, baby. One hundred percent.'

'That's what I'm talking about, sista-girl,' Roxy chimed in, reaching her hand through from the back and slapping skin with Lori.

For all her hippy-dippiness, Lori was no Polly-Anna. She'd been growing Marijuana long before Abby could even spell it. She'd messed with Ouija Boards and Tarot cards and all kinds of scary-ass shit that made a good Baptist girl like Abby more than a little nervous. Still, Lori was Abby's best bud and had been for as long as they both remembered. They were as different as day and night, but Lori was always there for her.

Abby looked out the window again, her eyes finding the woods. The tree branches were like limbs, all bent out of shape, scrambling to escape. She still had a weird feeling about this place. The woods, the lake, Black Water in general. Abby was meant to be getting away from it all, clearing her head, kicking back and having some fun. So why did she feel so damn tense?

Abby leaned her head against the car window, closed her eyes and tried to block everything out for a moment.

It was a year ago, today...

She'd been coming home from the gym, tired, hungry and in desperate need of a shower. She lived on the edge of town, five bucks in a cab, give or take. But that night Abby walked, enjoying the light breeze in the air.

She climbed the steps towards her apartment, lugging the gym bag behind her. There was a sound from outside, some car alarm going off. Abby had paused to look out the stairwell windows and saw a couple of youths running from the parking lot. She remembered sighing, shaking her head, recalling what her mother had said about living in the city.

She found her apartment and that familiar sense of dread bubbled up from within.

This is your home too, she reminded herself, before sliding her key into the lock and turning. Then she entered, dropped her bag in the hallway and reached for the light switch.

The first blow struck her face, the second to her stomach, winding her and dropping her to her knees. When she looked up, she found Danny. He'd been drinking. His breath reeked of alcohol. A crazed glint escaped bloodshot eyes.

Abby tried to pull away, but Danny grabbed her, leaning in close to her face. He screamed at her, asking where she was until now, which of those bastards she was sleeping with. He rhymed off people she would talk about from work, men she was meant to be fucking. Abby remembered feeling sick, bile building in the back of her throat like thick oil.

He dragged her to the living room, threw her onto the sofa. Then he hit her again and again. And it wasn't like other times: there was a look in his eye that was insatiable. He'd have killed her right there and then only Abby struck lucky, kicking him really hard between the legs and fleeing to the kitchen.

That was where she found the knife.

'Hey, Sleeping Beauty.'

Abby woke with a start. Lori was smiling over at her.

'Hey,' Abby said, removing her wireframes, rubbing her eyes, and then replacing them. The car had stopped by a clearing in the woods. 'This it, then?'

'Pretty much,' Lori said. 'Home, sweet home. Well, for the weekend, anyway.'

Abby stifled a yawn, looked around.

'So, what happens now?' Abby asked.

'Now,' Lori said, 'we meet Nanna and Gramps.'

Grandparents. That was exactly what Abby needed. The wholesome innocence of Southern-fried grandparents with their dungarees and earthy wisdom and home-cooked remedies for every ailment under the sun.

She climbed out of the car.

The sounds of the wild filled the air. The sun was red-hot, towering above the forest like some angry God. The Louisiana Oaks huddled closer now, thrust upward from the earth, standing shoulder-to-shoulder, branches twisted into painful claws poised to scratch the sky. The foliage formed a busy canopy that fought against the sun's glare, casting shadows upon the ground. Abby took a moment to breathe in the fresh country air. She closed her eyes, pitched her face to the sky.

Good air in, bad memories out. And repeat.

When she opened her eyes, Abby found Roxy smoking by a nearby tree. The other girl looked radiant. Her blonde hair was glowing, fluttering in the light breeze. One hand thumbed the belt loop of her denim skirt. A t-shirt knotted at the side revealed a glimpse of her taut belly.

'Hey,' she shouted over at Abby before blowing a cloud of smoke into the air.

'You ladies wanna help me with this stuff?' Lori called, head buried in the trunk of her car.

Roxy dropped her cigarette, trod it into the dust. She walked towards the car and Lori handed her a bunch of flexible poles.

'What's all this shit?' Roxy asked.

'Tent poles,' Lori replied, matter-of-factly.

'Yes, I know what they are,' Roxy snapped. 'Just don't know why *we* need them. We're staying in your nanna's cabin, right?'

'Wrong,' Lori said, pulling a heavy canvas bag from the trunk and slinging it over her shoulder. 'There ain't enough room. We're camping.'

'What?!' Roxy barked. 'I thought your folks were away this weekend.'

'They were *supposed* to go to my Aunt's, but Gramps came down with something Thursday night. So they're still here.'

'And you were going to tell us this *when*?!' Roxy fumed. She wasn't the outdoors type at all. Roxy's idea of roughing it was taking the bus into town.

Lori dipped her hands back into the trunk. 'It slipped my mind,' she said.

'It slipped your *freaking* mind?!'

'Come on, Roxy, this weekend's important.' Lori glanced towards Abby then raised her eyebrows. 'Look, it's a real nice tent. Sleeps four comfortably so there'll be plenty of room.'

Roxy blew some air out. 'Shit,' she said, then stormed back to the tree trunk and lit up again.

Abby looked down at her feet.

Lori walked over and placed a hand on her shoulder. 'Look,' she said. 'We're going to have a good time, okay? You know Roxy. She'll be fine once we break out the booze and Mary J.'

'I know,' Abby said. 'It's not Roxy I'm worried about. It's *me*, Lori. You've been so nice putting this all together, but I don't know if I'm up for it this weekend. I'm not in the partying mood. And this place…' She stared again towards the woods, rising up from the ground like jagged teeth. 'Something don't feel right. It's like I'm not meant to be here, Lori. Like the woods or the water or the sun don't want me here.'

'Nonsense,' Lori said. 'You think I wouldn't pick up on shit like that? I mean, *hello! Witchy Girl here!*' 'She smiled, threw an arm around Abby. 'Just you leave me to look after the mumbo-jumbo. You, girl, concentrate on getting your *mojo* back.'

'Never mind my mojo,' Abby said. 'I just wanna be able to close my eyes without seeing... *him.'*

A high-pitched scream rang out from the path up ahead.

Abby turned sharply, finding a rotund old black woman in a long white night dress and Bugs Bunny slippers bounding towards them.

'Nanna!' Lori sang. She left Abby, running to embrace the old woman.

'My, my, girl, how you've grown up,' Nanna said, sizing Lori up, eyes searching every inch of her lithe body. 'Such a skinny little thing. We gotta put some meat on them bones.' She turned to Abby, her smile revealing stained false teeth. 'Now, who would this be?'

'Nanna, this is Abby.'

'Well, I'm very pleased to meet you, young Abby,' Nanna said. But she wasn't pleased. Not one bit. She stood back from Abby suspiciously, one eyelid flickering.

Abby extended a handshake. 'Pleased to meet you, Miss...'

'Sawyer,' Nanna said, limply taking Abby's hand. 'And it's Mrs if it's all the same to you, Abby. I ain't footloose and fancy free like all you young'uns. Been married to Lori's Gramps for goin' on sixty years.'

Abby smiled, looked to Lori. 'Wow,' she said. 'Sixty years.'

Lori wrapped Nanna in her arms, leading her to the cabin. 'So how is Gramps?' she asked.

'Oh, he's fine. Nothing wrong with him. Likes to moan, so he does.'

'Lemme guess. The campground's got 'em all salty?'

'That and all this Christie Keller foolishness.'

'*Who's Christie Keller?*' Abby mouthed to Lori behind Nanna's back.

'*I'll tell ya later,*' Lori mouthed back.

Nanna shot a glance towards Roxy, still standing by the tree trunk, still smoking. 'Don't be littering my yard with them butts, young lady,' she barked.

Roxy rolled her eyes then took another drag.

Lori shook her head and laughed. 'Come on, Rox,' she called. 'I want y'all to meet Gramps.'

TWO

The cabin was set on a patch of open plain surrounded by a wall of oak trees. A small barn sat behind it, looking in need of some serious TLC. In the grass, at the base of the cabin, ran a border of thrift store kitsch with some sort of weird religious theme.

The girls walked up alongside the cabin, Lori leading the way. Roxy hooked her thumb at standouts jutting out from a busy ensemble of knickknacks and figurines in the grass. She made a face at Abby who just shrugged back at her. Around front, the porch was similarly cluttered. A row of herbs grew in large pots lined along the railing of the porch, partially obscuring the view of the plain and the trees that bordered it some one hundred feet back.

Roxy all but slammed into the body slumped on the porch swing. She let out a gasp and thrust herself away from it, nearly causing

Abby, who was a couple of paces behind her, to fall down the porch steps.

'WhathafuckisTHAT?!'

'Geez,' Abby breathed. 'What *is* that?'

The life-sized dummy was made of burlap stuffed with rags and dressed like an old railroad hobo. Its clothing, a P-coat, white dress shirt, black pants and work boots, was caked in dirt and stiff from years of baking in the Louisiana sun. One gloved hand held a sugar-cane knife, the other closed around a clutch of wilting flowers. The burlap man looked just like Abby felt: deflated. Its slumped head bore no features, a dome of coarse cloth with some strange writing scribbled in red ink. A necklace of bound chicken feet dangled from its neck. Another necklace constructed from beads hung slightly lower.

'Oh, that's just Geordi,' Lori shrugged, having glanced around to see what all the fuss was about.

'Geordi?' Roxy remained a safe distance from the porch swing, sizing its occupant up.

Lori laughed, walked over and sat next to the burlap dummy. She put her arm around it, drew the thing closer and said, 'How can you not love ol' Geordi?'

'What's it like a scarecrow or something?' Abby said.

'And what's all that writing on his face?' Roxy added.

'It's called a fetish,' Lori explained. 'Sort of like a scarecrow. You put it in front of your house to ward off evil spirits. The writing is just a bunch of Creole incantations and African glyphs. It's supposedly written in blood.'

'Hooo-lee shit, girl,' Roxy shuddered. 'You country folk are *seriously* weird.'

'Roxy!' Abby chided.

But Lori just laughed. 'Believe me, he used to freak me out, too, when I was a kid. I tried to de-creepify him with the flowers.' She ran her finger through them, rhyming off their names: 'Magnolias, azaleas, wild iris, and Cajun hibiscus. Gramps still replaces 'em with fresh ones when the old ones die. Isn't that sweet of him?'

'The whole thing actually seems kinda creepy to me,' Roxy said.

Nanna's voice filtered out through the screen door of the cabin. 'You girls comin' in or what?'

Lori pulled open the screen door and held it for Roxy and Abby. The two girls stepped tentatively over the threshold.

The interior of the cabin was small. Everything was compact. The first room they entered was the kitchen yet also acted as a dining room *and* living room. There was wood everywhere, pots and pans and clocks pinned liked badges to each logged wall. Above the fireplace hung a deer's head; eyes staring dead ahead as if the poor thing could still see himself out there in the woods, nosing that last bit of foliage.

They followed Nanna up the stairs, across the narrow landing, and past an open door leading into a small room with a red carpet. Against one wall, Abby noticed what looked to be an altar of some sort.

She made eyes at Roxy but Nanna hurried

them along before they could ask any more awkward questions.

Gramps was in the master bedroom, propped up on his four poster like some old king. He wore pale colored pajamas. The top buttons were undone, revealing thin, downy chest hair and an old pouch dangling from a rope around his neck. He was just about the blackest man Abby had ever seen. His skin was firewood, his eyes hidden behind a pair of dark sunglasses. He smiled as they came into the room, lips parting to reveal cream colored teeth.

Gramps sniffed the air, then spoke, his voice deep and wheezy: 'Who you got there for us, Elle. Is that our girl, Lori?'

'Sure is, Gramps,' Lori said, smothering him with a hug. 'Oh, I've missed you!'

Gramps patted Lori's back, face beaming with delight. He pointed the blackened lenses of his glasses across the room, seeming to find the other girls. 'And you brought your friends.' He sniffed again. 'Beautiful young girls, the two of them.'

'Abby and Roxy,' Lori said, looking at each of them in turn, 'this is Gramps.'

'Good to meet you, sir,' Abby said, stepping forward. She glanced at Nanna and smiled, but the old woman still eyed her suspiciously. 'This is, er, a lovely place you have,' she said, even though she didn't really think it. Even though the trees with their clawed fingers, and this little Voodoo shack spooked the hell out of her.

Gramps shrugged as if he'd never really thought about it. 'Keeps the rain out.'

'But that view,' Abby pressed, looking to the window. 'Must be great waking up to that every day.'

'Well, 'dem woods *smell* mighty fine this time of year, that's for sure. Of course, I haven't *seen* a damn thing in ten years.' He lifted the lenses from the bridge of his nose revealing eyes like two smooth pebbles under frosted glass.

Lori smiled meekly at Abby. 'Gramps's blind,' she said.

'Oh,' Abby said. She could feel her face redden. 'I'm sorry, I didn't know.'

'And who's your other friend?' Gramps cut in. He sniffed again.

'Er, Roxy,' the other girl said flatly. Her arms were folded, her lips upturned slightly at the corners. 'Hi,' she added, clearly no interest in any of this.

'Roxy, eh? Well, Roxy, you smell like bines if you don't mind me saying so. His nose danced with anticipation. 'You got some bines for an old man?' His eyes turned in his wife's general direction.

'Now don't you be letting him smoke,' the old woman scolded. 'He's terror for them bines!'

Lori looked to her friend, playing along with Nanna.

Roxy just shrugged. 'Okay,' she said. 'No bines for Gramps.'

Gramps turned to the old woman and frowned. 'Now you know you ain't right,' he sulked.

'You can tell me again how *I ain't right* when

16

you're waiting for your supper this evening,' Nanna smirked.

'See how she does me?' Gramps said to the girls.

They laughed along politely.

Then Lori's face changed. 'Outside you mentioned something about Christie Keller,' she said to Nanna.

'She did, did she?' Gramps perked up.

Nanna rolled her eyes, complained, 'Now you went and got him started.'

'It's those *damn fools* at that *damn fool* campgrounds!' Gramps barked. 'Good-fer-nothin's come up here looking to stir things up.'

'Whaddayou mean?' Lori said.

Abby and Roxy shared a quizzical look.

'Your grandpa chased away a group of kids messin' round with an Ouija board down by the lake a whiles back,' Nanna butted in.

'Damn straight,' Gramps added.

'There've been a few incidents where folks've claimed to have seen that poor girl, Christie Keller, of late. Ever since that write-up in that supermarket rag the kids like to read. Campground's been doing boomin' business because of it. Prob'ly them who's behind the whole thing.'

'So you say,' the old man grumbled defiantly, and for a moment or two they bickered like an old married couple. Gramps was of the opinion that the sightings were real while Nanna suspected a conspiracy concocted to bring business to the new Black Water Campgrounds. None of it was of any interest to Roxy who nudged Abby and made a play for the door.

But Lori grabbed her arm.

'Hold yer horses, girl. *Damn*!'

'So what they doin' here, these young' uns?' the old man asked. 'I'm sure they ain't here just to visit me.'

The girls looked up to find Gramps smirking at them knowingly

'They meant to stay here, mind the place while we were away,' Nanna said.

'Away where? We ain't goin' nowhere,' the old man spat.

'No, but we were *supposed* to go to Aunt Sally's,' Nanna reminded him. 'Only you were under the weather.'

'Ah,' the old man said. 'I was, wasn't I?'

He looked sad for a moment, then said, 'Sure there's plenty of room for them downstairs.' He looked in Roxy's direction, smiled, then added, 'And I got a place right here for that one.'

Roxy stepped back, horrified.

The old man laughed vicariously, as if he could see the expression on Roxy's face. But then he stopped, his face suddenly strained. A damp patch spread across the bed sheets in front of him, the distinct smell of urine filling the room.

'Oh, what you gone and done!' Nanna chastised, rushing to the bed and pulling the covers back. 'All these young girls in your room. Got you all excited, made you mess the bed! Didn't I just change that yesterday?!'

Roxy's eyes widened, color draining from her face.

Lori grabbed her arm. 'Okay, now we go,' she said, looking also to Abby. 'Come on!'

THREE

The three girls clambered down the old stairs and out the door.

They could still hear the old woman's voice as she scolded. Gramps protested uselessly, his wife's voice beating him down every time.

'Old folks,' Lori said, laughing. 'Gotta love 'em.'

Roxy was dumbfounded. 'What … *the fuck*?!'

'Oh, come on,' Lori countered. 'What do you expect? Living out here all alone?'

'I expected them to be *gone*,' Roxy argued. 'I expected a nice clean cabin. Somewhere to drink, smoke and play a little music. I expected what you *told* me to expect. What I *didn't* expect was to come out to the middle of nowhere and watch some ninety year-old piss himself!'

'Eighty-six,' Lori corrected. 'And I think he looks great for his age.'

Roxy laughed, threw her arms in the air. 'Whatever!'

'What's that pouch he's got around his neck?' Abby asked keen to change the subject.

'It's called a grigri bag,' Lori said, still shooting daggers at Roxy. 'Supposedly he's got some of Christie Keller's hair in there."

'Ewww. What would he want with a dead girl's hair?'

'For protection and to bring good luck. Grigri bags are pretty common in Voodoo.'

'Voodoo? But I thought you were into *witchcraft*?' Abby all but whispered the word.

'Wicca,' Lori corrected. 'But Gramps and

Nanna were brought up on Voodoo. It's in their blood. They never forced it on Mom; she went her own way when it came to religion and shit. Never talked much about it, to be honest.' Lori gave a shrug. 'Voodoo's alright but I like my magic more airy.'

Abby fumbled nervously with her hands. 'Are they… different; Wicca and Voodoo?'

Lori shook her head. 'Girlfriend, we need to get you an education on world religion. This is the '80s, darling. Time to get your head out of a hymn book and take a look around you.'

'Well, here's what I believe,' Roxy cut in. 'I believe in telling your friends *the truth*.'

'And what does that mean?' Lori retorted.

'Look, let's get the tent up,' Abby said quickly.

Lori blew some air out, glared at Roxy and mumbled something under her breath. She turned, looked across to the old barn, thought for a moment. 'We could set up camp in there,' she said. Her eyes found Roxy again. 'It ain't the cabin, but it's still technically indoors.'

'I'm not camping anywhere *near* this place,' Roxy fumed.

Lori exhaled in defeat. 'You know what, Roxy…'

'Okay, okay,' Abby jumped in. 'Please, no more fighting. I mean, surely there's somewhere else we can set up? What about the Campgrounds?'

'They're booked solid,' Lori said. 'I tried.'

'Well, that's just wonderful,' Roxy scoffed.

Lori glared at Roxy again then took a deep breath. 'There's a real nice spot on the edge of the forest, near the lake. It's a short hike from here. We can camp there.'

'You sure there's no weird Voodoo Shrine to the animal spirits or something out there that you wanna tell us about?' Roxy chided.

'Dammit Roxy!' Lori vented. 'I'm sorry! Okay? I didn't know they were gonna be here. And as far as the "weird Voodoo stuff" is concerned, it's no different than putting a statue of Jesus or the Virgin fucking Mary on your front lawn, or wearing a cross for that matter.'

'Please, Roxy,' Abby begged, really at the end of her tether. 'Let's just find a spot and get set up before it gets dark out, huh?'

Roxy stood there pouting, then exhaled and stormed towards the car. She dipped into the trunk, reached inside to pull out a canvas bag, looked again at the others. 'Well, come on then! What are you waiting for? Come on!'

Lori shook her head then moved to lift some poles.

Abby rolled her eyes then followed.

FOUR

The girls set up camp in a grassy alcove near the edge of the lake.

Roxy emptied the canvas bag she held containing the tent and other stuff. She pulled a bottle of spring water from one of the other bags, twisted the cap off, took a drink, and immediately spat it out.

'S'fucking warm,' she complained, wiping

her mouth. She put the lid back on the bottle and tossed it onto the pile of bags.

Lori walked up carrying a pair of tent poles, placed them on the ground near the contents of the canvas bag, and said, 'There's always the lake.'

'Oh, right,' Roxy scoffed. 'Drink from nature's toilet. No thanks.'

Still huffing, she fished a jacket and a pack of cigarettes from one of her bags, mumbled something about going to get some wood for the fire and stormed off.

Abby looked to Lori and sighed. She crouched over the various tent parts, trying to make sense of them. 'Where's the instructions for this thing?'

'Instructions? It's a friggin' tent,' Lori said. 'I thought you said your daddy used to take you camping?'

'That was ten years ago. And there was no way *my* daddy was gonna let his *little princess* get her hands dirty putting up a tent.'

Lori walked over and snatched the tent spike from Abby's hand. 'Gimme that.'

'Heyyyy!' Abby recoiled.

'The plan was for you to *relax* this weekend.'

'What? I can't put the tent together?'

'Apparently not?'

'Ha. *Ha*,' Abby said wryly as she rose to her feet. She stepped aside and made an "all yours" motion with her hands.

Lori got down on her knees and went to work.

Time passed. A tent was taking shape from the wrinkled tarp and flexible poles and spikes.

Abby stood by the edge of the lake looking out at the water.

'Beautiful, isn't it?' Lori called out to her.

'You know what, it really is,' Abby agreed, smiling, glad that her bad vibes about the place from earlier were lifting. 'The water's so calm. It kinda hypnotizes you if you stare too long.'

'Um hmm.'

'I feel like this is all my fault,' she added after a moment's introspection.

'What's your fault?'

'The mix-up with the cabin, Roxy getting mad…'

Lori stopped what she was doing. 'Look, it's not your fault, Abby,' she said. 'It was *my* grandparents that fucked everything up.'

Abby shrugged. 'Speaking of which. You said that you had no idea about their change of plans until we got here. But then you said that you tried to book us at the campground before we left. Now, why would you need to do that unless you already knew about—'

'Alright. I lied. I knew before we left,' Lori conceded. 'Please don't be pissed at me?'

'Of course I'm not pissed at you,' Abby said.

Lori sighed. 'Look, I never would've gotten you guys out here if I'da told you the truth.'

'Yeah… You're probably right.'

'I had good intentions.'

'I know you did, Lori. Roxy knows, too.'

'Oh, I'm not so sure about that. You don't know Rox like I do.'

Lori resumed erecting the tent, all the while complaining about Roxy: how stubborn and unreasonable she could be, how she always

23

seemed one step away from bitch-mode these days. She hammered the last peg of the tent in angrily, then stood back and admired her work.

'Done,' she announced, blowing some air out, waiting to accept congratulations.

When none came she whipped around, looking for Abby.

But Abby was nowhere to be seen.

Abby followed the jagged lake line, entranced by the cool-hand flow of black water. She hadn't meant to go so far. She'd hoped to run into Roxy, maybe set things right with her, but as her feet wandered so had her mind and before she knew it, twenty minutes and a lot of ground had passed. She stopped, deciding to get her bearings lest she get lost. Across the lake a staggered mass of oak stood on intertwined legs, exposed roots intertwined. Legions of reeds waded out into the shallow water.

She heard voices up ahead.

Abby stopped and listened. Two people. A man and a woman, Yankees by the sound of their accents.

She walked a little further, then a little more. The voices were louder now.

'But what if something goes wrong?' Abby heard the woman say.

'Nothing's gonna go wrong. Now just go,' an impatient male voice replied.

Gingerly, Abby drew closer.

The voices led her to a line of knock-kneed tree trunks bumping hips and playing foot-sie by the lake. She saw movement behind them. There was a loud 'click-clack' sound and then she heard the sound of someone wading through water.

Abby rose up onto the balls of her feet, turned her posture on sneak, and crept closer to the knock-kneed oaks.

She peeked through and saw a woman walking into the lake. She had tanned skin wrapped in a dark-colored tank top and raven hair that hung past her shoulders. She was already waist deep in the water but waded further in, like she meant to walk across to the other side. The woman took a deep breath when the water reached her face and then disappeared completely beneath the surface. A cluster of bubbles raged briefly before the water became still as glass.

Thirty seconds passed without as much as a ripple. Abby stared at the water, wondering if she should be worried or not. Had the woman got into trouble? Was this some sort of a suicide attempt? And hadn't she heard a male voice earlier? Had he abandoned her?

Abby ran out from behind the trees and started hopping out of her shoes. She focused on the spot where the woman went under, started wading in.

Movement in her periphery. Abby whipped her head around. Shrieked at the one-eyed, mecha-monstrosity lumbering near the water's edge.

'Jeeeeezus! Mary! And Joseph!' came a voice from behind a bulky JVC Camcorder. A tall slender man lowered the thing from his shoulder and walked out into the clearing. 'You ruined my shot!'

He was shirtless and built like a retired track athlete. Long, lean legs jutted out of powder-blue Adidas shorts. Honey-brown hair covered his chest. Abby felt her heart skip a beat. She suddenly felt very embarrassed.

'I don't understand,' she said, somewhat relived yet still confused.

'You ran right out in the middle of my shot!' the man said. 'Tha hell were you thinking?!'

'But the girl in the water?' Abby pointed at the lake.

The cameraman had a big ole walkie-talkie holstered on a military-style utility belt he wore around his waist. He pulled it out, held it up to his mouth, and spoke into the thing.

'Come on up,' he said.

There was a disturbance in the water. Seconds later a face pushed through the surface trailing hair as black as the lake itself. It was the woman Abby had seen walking into the lake. She was wearing goggles. Her lips were stretched around the mouthpiece of a snorkel. She whipped her hair out of her face and then noticed Abby standing there looking back at her. The goggles came off and she spat out the snorkel. She turned and glared at the tall, slender man.

'What's going on?' the woman said. 'And who the hell is *she*?'

'So, what's the movie about?' Abby asked Elaine Sedaris from Lansing Michigan.

'It's not a movie,' Elaine's husband Jeff cut in abruptly, seeming agitated. The Bartles and Jaymes t-shirt he had put on hung way past his

Adidas shorts and gave the illusion that he was naked underneath.

'Don't mind my husband,' Elaine said as she towelled off. She wore a navy blue bathing suit that hugged her slightly pear shape. 'He takes his craft *very* seriously.'

'Craft?' Abby said.

'Filmmaking.'

'Videography!' Jeff corrected her.

'Ex-*scuse* me.'

The Sedarises appeared older than Abby, but not by much. Maybe in their late twenties. Elaine had a mischievous air that came through in the way she held her face. Jeff was pretty one-note. Abrupt. Intense. Maybe a little nervous.

'We're shooting footage about the lake for the local News,' Jeff said to Abby. 'My wife was testing the lake for some underwater shots we're gonna do.'

The News? Abby was the darling of the local News just over a year ago. She wondered if the Sedarises might recognize her. But the Sedarises were Yankees, from well above the Mason Dixon Line. To them she was probably just another Southern Belle.

'Is there another campground around here?' Elaine said as she hiked a pair of jeans up her chunky hips and buttoned the fly. 'You and your friends aren't staying at the Stogies. I would've recognized a pretty-lil thing like you.'

'My friend Lori's grandparents have a cabin,' Abby said.

Jeff Sedaris' interest was suddenly piqued. 'Oh really? Whereabouts?'

'Why? You thinking about paying them a visit?' Elaine frowned.

Jeff glared at her. Elaine glared right back.

'Speaking of my friends,' Abby said, capitalizing on the awkward moment. 'I should probably get back to them.' *To tell them all about you two weirdos, for one.*

'Well. I'm sorry if we scared you,' Elaine said. '*Some*-body was supposed to make sure that the area was all clear.'

'*Some*-body did,' Jeff replied.

'It's okay,' Abby said.

There was a sound, like sticks breaking under foot. Seconds later an exotic beauty wearing Daisy-Dukes appeared from behind the oak trees looking worried and out of breath.

'Lori!' Abby's face lit up. Lori didn't return the same enthusiasm.

'Well. Look at that,' Elaine Sedaris grinned. 'The woods are just spittin' out pretty girls today.'

FIVE

A fucking tent!

Roxy had never stayed in one. Not even as a kid.

She may have visited the circus once. She could remember clowns at some stage in her life and that may have involved a tent. But this *camping* thing with its fires and sing-a-longs and marshmallows? Just wasn't her.

Truth of the matter was she was still mad at

Lori. She needed to be on her own for a while. Roxy wasn't used to being with people twenty-four-seven even at the best of times. Outside of the club she worked at, she kept to herself. And anyway, with the way Lori and Abby had been getting on, agreeing with one another and making her out to be a bitch, Rox was beginning to feel like the odd one out.

She didn't know Abby too well. Sure, she seemed a nice girl. But to Roxy, Abby would always be Danny's girlfriend, first and foremost. She knew all the shit that went down, or at least what was reported in the papers. And then there was the small matter of Roxy having slept with Danny. Nobody had brought it up yet but that just made things all the weirder. In fact, the more Roxy thought about it, the more freaked out she was about this whole scene.

Not to mention that weirdass burlap man and all the Voodoo bullshit…

Roxy wandered along the forest trail, heading back towards the road.

The sun had sneaked beneath the canopy roof of the forest. A dull hue spread across the dry clay path but it was still light enough to walk around for a while longer, Roxy figured, even without a flashlight.

She passed the car, still parked in the clearing, and headed on up the path towards the cabin. She found a tree looking out from the woods onto the plain and leaned against it, sparking up.

Her eyes traced the cabin, wondering what age it was, whether it was as old as its two occupants. Had the old man built it himself? Felling some trees, stacking the wood.

Roxy could see him in her head, much younger, standing by a tree stump, stooped over his axe, sweat lashing off his face. The image was almost romantic, lending the old shack a better light, and for the briefest of moments, Roxy could appreciate the beauty of the Great Outdoors. That mystical stuff Lori was spouting earlier, about being at one with nature, well maybe it wasn't all bullshit.

She smiled, shook her head. *Yeah right.*

Roxy Blue was a city girl through and through. She liked her home comforts too much to be anything else. This was a girl for whom make-up and patent shoes meant a hell of a lot more than the sound of birds singing, or water flowing through the damn forest. Give her a nice comfy bed any day to this camping BS.

She dropped one cigarette to the ground before sparking up another. Looked at her watch. It was getting dark much quicker than she had expected and Roxy guessed she would need to be getting back soon, grabbing that firewood she'd promised to get on the way.

She dragged on her newly lit cig, exhaling slowly.

Her eyes found the cabin again.

Its bedroom light snapped on. The old man was stood by the window, the blackened lenses of his sunglasses pointed right at her.

He smiled.

Roxy looked away. She tried to take another drag on her cigarette but her hand was shaking too much.

She looked up at the bedroom window again, but this time the old man was gone. Her eyes stayed on the house, searching for him, but he didn't come back. Finally, the bedroom light snapped off.

Roxy lowered her eyes and gasped at the sight of Geordi, the burlap man watching her from his post on the cabin porch.

'What're YOU looking at?!' she challenged, half-serious. Then shook her head, allowing herself a little laugh. *Geez, girl*, she mused. *All that Voodoo talk's messin' with your head. Old man's blind for Chrissakes! Can't see the foot of his bed, never mind out the window.*

She dropped the cigarette, stomping it into the ground with the heel of her cowboy boot, then made her way back down the path towards the car. She was just about to step into the clearing when something reached out from the trees, grabbing her.

SIX

Roxy pulled away, tripping on the hard mud of the dirt track and falling to the ground.

A tall man wearing a Stetson stepped out from the trees.

'Geez, girl, didn't mean to spook ye,' he said.

He removed the Stetson, offered his hand. Roxy allowed him to pull her up.

'John C. Lane at your service, Ma'am,' he said, replacing the Stetson.

'Well, you just scared the shit out of me,

31

John C.,' Roxy said, dusting herself down. 'Mind telling me why you're sneaking up on a girl like that?'

'Oh, I didn't mean nothin' by it,' John protested, hands raised, palms facing forwards. 'I'm here with some buddies. We're pitched about a mile from here, just north of the river. I was out for a wander, just now, when I spotted ye. You must be staying at the Stogie's, huh?'

'The who?'

'The new campground.'

'I wish.'

John C. hesitated. His eyes travelled up Roxy's legs, towards her hips. They found her breasts, his lips curling into a half-smile.

'Yer from the city ain't cha, Miss....'

Roxy folded her arms, drawing the cardigan closed over her t-shirt.

'Name's Roxy,' she said. 'And is it that obvious?'

'You, er, here alone, Miss Roxy?'

Roxy shifted uncomfortably. 'No, I'm camping with friends. And it's just Roxy.'

'My mistake,' John C. said, overplaying his contrition. His eyes still lingered on her chest, his face still twisted in that half-grin-half-sneer. 'Where you pitched, Roxy?'

'By the lake,' Roxy said, wishing immediately that she hadn't.

'The lake? You serious?'

'Why, what's wrong with the damn lake?'

John C. blew some air out, pushed the Stetson back in his hair. 'Ain't you 'fraid of that witch?'

'What witch?' Roxy asked, pretty much

ready to level him if he said Lori's name. Lori could be a royal pain in the ass sometimes but she was still a friend and Roxy wasn't for letting no-mark rednecks like John C. Lane here go mouthing about her friends.

'Christie Keller. The witch they drowned at the lake. They say that sometimes when the moon rises a certain way, it turns blood red and Christie comes out of the lake and possesses folk.'

Roxy sucked her teeth in response to the Keller girl's name. Wasn't that the same name the old man had been fretting over back at the cabin?

'What's wrong?' John C. asked.

'Nothing,' she said, straightening her face. 'You actually believe all that horseshit?'

'It's what folks round here believe,' John C said. 'Christie Keller was a real person. Years ago she supposedly possessed some folks back in town, made them do all sorts-a-terrible things, so they took her up to the lake and did the witch test on her.'

'The what test?'

'You never heard of the witch test? Basically, they dunked you under the water three times. If you drowned, well that meant you weren't a witch. But if you popped back up after the third time, well then you *was* a witch and needed to be dealt with accordingly.'

'You mean like the Salem Witch Trials?'

'That's right. Same thing happened here in Black Water.'

'Bullshit,' Roxy said. 'That's just some old campfire tale to scare all the locals. Every town's got one.'

John C. winked. 'If you say so, missy.'

'Look, I need to get going,' Roxy said.

'I'll walk with you.'

'No you fucking won't,' Roxy corrected him.

'You sure about that? The woods can be a dangerous place for a woman to be walking alone—specially a fine looking thing like yerself.'

'Excuse me?'

'Just being gentlemanly is all.'

Roxy took a moment to size up John C. Tall, broad shouldered and not at all bad looking were you to go for that redneck Momma's Boy kinda schtick. But she wasn't fooled by his routine.

She shook her head and sighed. 'Gentlemanly, huh? Heard that one before. Y'all are real gentlemen until you get what you want. Right?'

John C. laughed. 'Can't blame a guy for trying.'

Roxy back-stepped towards the woods shaking her head at the cowboy's patter.

'Last chance,' he said.

'A little piece of advice; learn how to talk to girls,' Roxy offered.

'You don't know what you're missing.'

'In your dreams.'

'Maybe I'll see you again?' John C. called after her.

'Not if I see you first,' Roxy said, disappearing down the trail.

***

'Hey-ho,' John C. said as he wandered into the improvised campsite.

A single tent was pitched in the centre walled in by the rampant undergrowth. The small clearing appeared man-made, and done so with haste.

In the middle of the campsite, a charred carcass hung on a spit. It was mostly stripped to the bone. A fire simmered beneath it. A bucket rested on the ground near the tent, a long haired man stripped to the waist, scooping handfuls of water over his torso. Blood was dried into his hands, arms and face.

He looked up as John C. Lane made his entrance and asked, 'Where have you been?'

'Took a stroll,' John replied. 'Trail leads out the other side of the forest towards some old cabin.'

'I didn't know there were folks living way out here,' the long haired guy replied.

'Sure looks like it. And that ain't all.' There was a glint in John's eye as he talked. 'Ran into this girl. And, man, she's a honey. Blonde hair, tits,' John made a gesture with his hands, estimating the size. 'Real beaut.'

'You're kidding me,' a third man said, unrolling the flap of the tent and dipping his head out. He was chewing as he spoke. In his hand was a half empty bowl and fork. A pair of Mossy Oak Hunting Binoculars dangled from his neck. He looked cleaner cut than the other two. Younger, good skin, preppy looking clothes. 'Was she alone?'

'Not exactly,' John C. said. 'She's got two buddies with her. No doubt hotties like she is. Good looking girl like that ain't gonna be hangin' out with no hounds.'

Nodding approvingly as he chewed his food, Preppy said, 'She better-looking than the housewife?'

The guys had met a husband and wife while hunting a few days ago. Apparently the couple had gotten themselves lost while out filming some news thing and were trying to find their way back to the Stogie's campground. The guys had been regaling the fuckability of the raven-haired housewife ever since, and the likelihood that the husband wasn't meeting her needs, so to speak.

'Speak for yourself,' Long-Hair said. 'That plump ass-a-hers'll do me just fine.'

'Where these girls camped then?' Preppy pressed, placing the bowl to the ground then washing down his chow with a swig from his flask.

'Down by the lake, she said.'

'No shit,' Preppy almost spat out his drink. 'The lake where Christie Keller was drowned?'

'Must be,' Long Hair broke in, shaking the excess wetness from his hands. 'That's the only lake around these parts.' Most of the blood had been scrubbed from his skin. He ran one hand through his scraggy hair, flicked it away from his eyes. 'I like the sound of this girl,' he added, dropping the soap into his bag and reaching for a towel. 'And these friends of hers?' He sat himself down by the fire, found a pack of cigarettes and lit one. 'Well, ain't that more for the takin'.'

'I thought you were good with the housewife's plump ass?' Preppy ribbed.

'There comes a point when rubbing one out while you boys are asleep just don't cut it.'

'Tell me you didn't,' John C. said.

'Sure did,' Long-Hair said proudly. 'Last couple nights. Gotta get rid of that poison, right?'

The other two laughed.

'You horny bastard,' John C. said shaking his head.

'That's right,' Long Hair responded. 'And I ain't ashamed to admit it, neither.'

Preppy gestured to the carcass on the spit with his flask and said, 'Can't waste good meat.'

'Ain't that the truth,' Long Hair agreed, smiling. He nodded towards the forest then looked back at John C., his face suddenly serious. 'So tell us more about these girls of yours,' he said.

SEVEN

It was full-on dark by the time Roxy reached the lake. The other two girls sat on the ground outside the tent, a campfire burning brightly. The water stretched beyond them, total darkness that went on for as far as the eye could see.

'Geez, girl,' Lori piped up. 'Where you been?'

'Getting firewood,' Roxy said, dropping a handful of wood to the ground. 'Guess you don't need it.'

Lori shrugged, lifted a joint to her lips. She took a long hit and held in the smoke.

''Ere,' she said, offering Roxy the joint. Her eyes looked red and watery in the firelight.

'Don't mind if I do,' Roxy said, taking the joint and sucking on it. She fixed the other girls a look. 'Got the tent up, I see,' she said, releasing the smoke.

'Thanks to Lori,' Abby replied. She wore an oversized sweatshirt and had been wearing jeans all day, despite the heat. The round wireframes rested low on the bridge of her nose. To Roxy, she looked like a little bird perched there on the ground.

'Yeah. While you were off making new friends,' Lori said to Abby.

'New friends?' Roxy quizzed.

'Oh, just some people that're staying at the campground,' Abby said.

Lori raised an eyebrow. 'Ms. Technically Challenged over here went for a little walk while I was putting up the tent. She walks down there a ways, looking for you apparently, when she hears something.' Lori looked at Abby. 'Right?'

Abby smiled weakly.

'Well. What'd you hear?' Roxy said.

Abby took the reins reluctantly. 'It sounded like a man and a woman, not really arguing, but bickering, like,' she said. 'So, naturally, I decided to take a look.'

'*Naturally*,' Lori said, rolling her eyes. 'Without telling me, of course. I was worried sick, you know.'

'Just let her finish,' Roxy protested.

'So, I followed the voices to this clearing on the edge of the lake,' Abby said. 'I peeked out from behind some trees and saw this woman literally walking into the lake until she was, like, completely under the water.'

Roxy looked to Lori, who validated Abby's story with a nod then added, 'I wouldn't have believed it if I didn't see them for myself.'

'Then what happened?'

'So, I start hopping out of my shoes thinking that I'm gonna have to go in and rescue this chick or else she's gonna drown. I'm just about to go in when this guy comes outta nowhere, cussin' and carryin' on about how I ruined his shot. He's got this big ole video camera on his shoulder. Turns out they were filming stuff for the News. The wife was checking the lake 'cause I guess they're gonna do some underwater filming or whatever.'

'You saw this, too?' Roxy asked Lori.

'Hell yeah. I met them; Elaine and Jeff...' Lori struggled to remember their last name.

'Sedaris,' Abby said.

'Sedaris. That's it.'

'They seemed pretty cool,' Abby cut in. 'A little weird, maybe. But it takes all kinds, right?'

'*Hey*, that's my line,' Lori scolded.

'I guess it is,' Abby grinned. 'Maybe you're starting to rub off on me.'

Abby and Lori laughed.

'And here I thought I had the big news,' Roxy said.

'Don't tell me,' Lori quipped. 'You found a Five Star Hotel?'

'No. Smartass. But I did find something.'

'Well, out with it,' Lori said.

'Some guys camping up the river.'

'Yeah?' Lori said.

'Yeah. Met one of them out by the cabin. Not bad looking if you're into the creepy wannabe cowboy type.'

'Okaaay,' Lori laughed. 'You can have that one.' She winked at Abby. 'Maybe there'll be another two more our types.'

'No way,' Abby said. 'The last thing I need is some guy this weekend.'

'Times two,' Roxy said. 'We're on vacation, right? So no guys for this girl.'

'You've got to be kidding me,' Lori protested. 'Vacation *means* cute guys. Look it up in the dictionary.'

'Not to me it doesn't,' Roxy said. 'I see guys all day every day. Some of them are even cute, but it's still work.'

Abby looked confused.

'I'm a stripper, honey,' Roxy told her. 'Didn't Lori tell you?'

'Stripper *with extras*,' Lori added, making a jerking-off gesture with her right hand.

Abby looked horrified.

Lori raised her eyebrows at Roxy then changed the subject. 'So you walked all the way back to the cabin?'

'Sure did,' Roxy said. She took another hit, handed the joint back. 'Felt like a spare tit around you two.'

'Oh come on,' Lori protested, taking the joint. 'Don't be like that, Rox!'

'Don't be like *what*?! You know it's true. You two go back years.'

'Sure, but we need you, Roxy. You're the party girl, everyone knows that. Without you, we'd end up behaving ourselves around here.'

Roxy fell suddenly quiet. She stared into the flames, watching them dance around the wood.

'Hey, what's wrong?' Lori asked.

'Is that how people see me?' Roxy said, eyes still fixed on the fire.

'What? The party girl? Sure!' Lori said. 'You're our rock n' roll queen! The groupie with the groove!'

Roxy smiled thinly. 'Right,' she said.

'Oh come on!' Lori protested. 'What have I done now?'

'Nothing,' Roxy said. 'Just don't want people thinking bad of me.'

'Nobody thinks bad of you,' Lori said. 'You've just got a...' she searched for the right word, '*spark* about you, yeah? I told you, girl, that's why we want you here.' She smiled, raised her hands to the sky. 'You light us up, babe.'

'And I could do with a little lighting up, in case you hadn't noticed,' Abby added meekly.

The girls continued smoking and chatting as the firelight bounced around the campsite illuminating the large, dome-shaped tent and the partially bald clearing. The trees leaned towards them in the light breeze, seeming to eavesdrop. The music of the night suggested a world unseen, things with spiny exoskeletons, long, hairy legs, and mouths with too many moving parts scurrying beyond the firelight's reach. Roxy shuddered at the different sounds and complained that she didn't want to wake up to some giant fucking insect crawling on her.

'Could you blame them for trying to cop a feel?' Lori joked.

Abby stifled a laugh.

Roxy shrugged, totally not taking the bait. 'I'm probably going to regret bringing this up,' she began, changing the subject. 'But that guy I mentioned earlier? The redneck with the Stetson? Well, it sounded like he drank the same Kool Aid as your grandpa.'

Lori's eyes narrowed. 'Huh?'

'He got all bent outta shape when I told him that we were camping by the river,' Roxy continued. 'Started going on and on about Christie fucking Keller. So, is everybody around here crazy over this chick or something?'

'Oh yeah,' Abby said to Lori, her face lighting up. 'You were supposed to tell me about that.'

'Ah, it's just an old urban myth,' Lori said. 'Christie Keller was this local girl they drowned in the lake for being a witch. Messed around with people's heads, they say, and made them do terrible things. None of it was true, though. Just your typical Salem bullshit. But she's become a bit of a bogeyman around these parts. Folks tell their kids that every once in a while the moon turns blood red and ol' Christie'll possess their ass if they're badly behaved.'

Abby's eyes widened. She hooked a thumb. 'Wait a minute. They drowned her in a lake? You mean *that* lake?'

Lori raised an eyebrow. 'Ain't no other lakes round here.'

Roxy laughed. 'This trip just gets better and better.'

'Ah, you ain't got nothin' to worry about,

Rox,' Lori said. 'You being as pure as the driven snow an' all.'

A toad protested in baritone.

Abby shrieked and jumped to her feet swatting at her hip, crying, 'Shit! Shit!'

'What's-a-matter?' Lori said.

But Abby kept swatting and spinning like a dog chasing its tail. She stopped. Looked down at her hip.

'A spider was crawling up my leg,' she said. 'I think I got it.'

Lori shook her head and laughed, and then she saw Roxy, who had skittered away on her butt and was now sitting at the edge of the campsite, her face almost lost in the darkness.

Lori waved a hand. 'Ah, you guys just crack me up,' she scoffed.

Roxy lifted an old doobie butt and threw it at Lori in jest. Abby laughed along.

The night's song grew louder.

Just behind the treeline, the moon turned a subtle shade of pink.

EIGHT

Roxy woke to find herself lying on the ground, looking up. She had dozed off. It was pitch-dark now, the trees all but blending into the clear, starlit skies. The night songs continued, which seemed normal enough before the mental fog settled and the distant sound of a harmonica wailing a bluesy riff began to register.

Roxy sat up and found Abby standing a

few feet away with heavy arms. Her head was crooked to the side and she was staring up at the sky, seemingly entranced by the harmonica's haunting echo.

'Please tell me I'm dreaming,' was the first thing out of Roxy's mouth.

'Nope,' Abby said without looking.

'What the hell is that?' Roxy complained.

'Lori's grandpa,' Abby said flatly.

'Why am I not surprised?' Roxy muttered, glaring at Lori who was curled up in her sleeping bag by the campfire, snoring. 'Figures she'd sleep right through it.'

'Too much Mary,' Abby quipped. 'Plus, she's probably used to it. Supposedly the old man does this every night.'

Roxy picked herself up, walked over, and stood next to Abby in the middle of the clearing, underneath the wailing black sky. 'She sure is full of surprises, that girl, ain't she?'

'That she is.'

The harmonica sang a while longer. The forest's own music was all but winding down, save for the occasional cricket and an owl singing acapella. The owl's forlorn calling should have spooked Roxy but right now she couldn't seem to give a shit. Thanks to grandpa and his spooky-ass harmonica solo. Thanks to the dying campfire singing its throaty country song. And thanks to the dope still working its way through her system.

'Now where'd Ole Mary get off to?' Roxy said, scanning the area as they sat down on the ground in front of the dying campfire.

Abby still had a half-dead roach pinched

between her fingers. She held it up and made a "Ta Da!" face. She fished a lighter from her pocket, lit the end, took a long drag, and then passed it to Roxy on the exhale.

Roxy put the roach to her lips and inhaled deep.

She turned to Abby. 'Tell me what happened that night,' she said in a delicate tone. 'With Danny. I mean, I know *what happened*. I read the papers, listened to the gossip round town. The bitches at the club were all abuzz about it.' She fixed Abby a look. 'But I never heard *your* side before.'

'That's because I never said anything after it happened,' Abby said, her face growing tight. 'Too busy lying in bed with the blankets over my head, wishing to God I could die. Stayed like that for a whole week. Never ate, didn't go out. Just stayed there in bed, wearing the same clothes.'

'This was afterwards?' Roxy said.

'This was *during*,' Abby said. 'From the night it happened.'

'Jesus,' Roxy muttered.

'His body was in the other room,' Abby said, her voice suddenly hoarse. 'But I forgot all about it after a while. They said it smelled so bad that the neighbours reported it. The cops came knocking but I can't remember any of that.'

Neither girl spoke for a while. The woods were quiet, all their singing done, the trees seeming to hang on Abby's every word now. There was no harmonica. The fire was but a dull glow. Roxy pulled her knees up to her chest, cupping her hands as if to pray, and looked to the sky.

'Look, I know you don't believe me,' Abby said suddenly.

'What?'

'About Danny. You don't believe me. You were with him before me, Roxy. I know all that.'

Roxy waved a hand. 'None of that matters,' she said.

'Matters to me,' Abby corrected.

'Really?'

'Yeah, really.' Abby caught a chill and snaked her hands into the extra-long sleeves of the sweatshirt. 'You can read all the papers you want but they don't tell you the half of it,' she spat. 'The endless questions, interviews, cross-examinations. They put me on trial, Roxy. They put *me* on trial for getting lucky and putting an abusive son of a bitch down before he killed me.'

'Abby, look, I—'

'You were lucky, Roxy. Lucky he didn't do to you what he did to me. And you know what the worst of it is?' Abby's eyes were watering now, her voice shaking. 'I still wonder why that is. Why the prosecution were able to produce witness after witness, every last one of them spewing on about what a stand-up Christian Danny was, model-fucking-citizen.'

Lori had woken up, unpeeling herself from the sleeping bag. She went to comfort Abby, but Abby pulled away. 'No,' she said, raising her hands as if threatened. She looked back to Roxy. 'You seem to know everything so tell me this, Roxy. Was it me? Did I draw all that rage out of him, somehow? TELL ME!'

'Abby, stop it!' Lori broke in.

'Stop *what*?!' Abby cried, tears breaking across her face. 'Stop thinking about him? Stop talking about him? Jesus, Lori, he's a part of me now! He's in my head, in my blood. He's all people think about when they see me. I can't get him out,' she wailed. 'I can't get him out.'

NINE

The moon stood tall and proud, casting its radiant gaze down at the lake. Abby sat outside alone staring at the horizon with naked eyes, wireframes hanging from her fingertips. She rubbed her tired eyes and then replaced the glasses.

She was on the edge of the clearing by the trees. She'd told the others she needed time to clear her head but that was, what, half an hour ago and her head was anything but clear. She was thinking about Danny. About what had happened last year and what it had done to her. Abby used to be normal. She used to be the kind of girl other girls' mothers looked at and wished they had as their own. But then Danny came along and changed all that. And now she was a crazy bitch, shouting at her friends and then storming off.

She heard a sound and turned to find Lori.

'Hey,' Lori said.

Abby smiled meekly. 'Hey.'

'That moon sure is beautiful,' Lori said, sidling up to her friend.

'Look, I said I should be alone,' Abby cut in.

'Bullshit,' Lori replied, sitting herself down next to Abby. 'Here, I made you this.'

Lori handed Abby a bracelet made of flowers.

'What is it?' Abby asked suspiciously. 'Some sort of charm?'

'No, it's some sort of daisy chain,' Lori said, smirking.

Abby laughed. She looked down at the flowers in her hand, gently stroking their tiny petals, then looked to her friend.

'I'm scared, Lori,' she said. 'I mean, *really* scared. How I was with you and Roxy earlier? That isn't me. You've known me since we were kids and that just isn't the way I normally act.'

Lori smiled. 'Look, what you went through was traumatic,' she said. 'So of course you're going to feel different after that. But it doesn't have to be bad. You can heal and move on from this a stronger person.'

'You think so?'

'Hell yeah.'

Lori seemed to think for a moment before adding, 'Hey, wanna try something?'

'Like what,' Abby said, cautiously.

'Like something that might help you.'

'What do you mean?' Abby's eyes brightened. 'Wait, do you have any Mary Jane left?'

'Nope. Not that. Something even *better*.' Lori went back to the tent. She returned with something in her hands, showed it to Abby. It was a book. Some New Age thing called *The Out of Body Experience*.

Disappointed, Abby scrunched her face and said, 'I'm not really into all that stuff, Lori. No offense.'

'Shhh,' Lori chided.

She shifted on the ground in order to face Abby. She opened the book, folded it and rested it on the ground by her side. She took Abby's hands in hers. 'Close your eyes,' she said.

'What are you—?'

'Just do it!'

Still reluctant, Abby did it, closing her eyes tight.

'Okay,' Lori said, 'I want you to clear your head.'

Abby laughed. 'Are you kidding me?'

'Seriously. Just think of nothing.'

Abby sighed. This was stupid. Yet despite herself, she did just as her friend asked, trying desperately to empty the chaos from her mind. She tried to move herself out of the forest, and away from the lake, but their darkness seemed to overshadow her.

'This isn't working,' she complained.

'You're in the bedroom of your old apartment,' Lori encouraged. 'It looks exactly how it did the night Danny attacked you.'

Abby sighed again, trying to imagine herself in her old apartment. She had since moved to a new apartment but the old place was still fresh in her mind.

She pictured the panelled bedroom door. That horrible '70s wallpaper. The red and white striped curtains. The cream colored carpet felt soft on her bare feet.

'The window's open,' Lori continued. 'It's

sunny out but there's a light breeze coming in.'

Abby looked to the window. The curtains, crumpled together like an accordion on either side, lifted and fell from the light breeze. Strangely, she could feel the breeze against her skin. Beyond the window, a seventh floor view across the city.

'You reach to close the window. You feel safe but want to make sure there's no way for anything to disturb you. You're blocking everything out, Abby. It's just you, alone in your room.

'There's a bed nearby.' Abby could see it. The diagonally striped duvet matched her curtains. It looked inviting, made to perfection with plump, puffed-out pillows. 'You climb into it. You're comfortable and feel safe and secure, so you close your eyes and start to fall asleep.'

Abby felt herself drift. Lori's voice disappeared into the background. Abby was tired for real after all that had happened, and all of the nervousness and stress seemed to go now, just like Lori had said it would. Her friend's voice was still there but further away. Even the sun was gone, the bedclothes soft and cool as they wrapped around her body and face.

Abby rolled over, stretching out, but her arm hit something and in the dream she opened her eyes.

Danny was in bed beside her.

Buried in his chest was the blade of the kitchen knife Abby had used. He smiled at her, his teeth bloodied.

'What's wrong?' he said, winking at her. 'Cat got your tongue?'

Abby jumped out of bed. 'No, this isn't happening,' she said, trying desperately to open her eyes – her real eyes – yet failing. She tried to focus on Lori's voice, but it was too far away, barely audible.

'She can't help you,' Danny said. 'No one can help you. It's just you and me, babe.'

He drew the knife from his chest, licked it clean of his own blood. 'Juicy,' he said, grinning. Then he sang into the knife-handle as if it were a microphone. 'Babe... dat dah, dat dah, dat dah, I got you, babe.'

Abby ran towards the window, pulling at the catch, but it was closed tight. The view was different from before, the window now looking out onto their campsite. Abby could see Lori, sitting in the clearing by the lake, holding her book.

And something else...

Geordi, that old burlap man from Nanna's porch, stood behind Lori, as if alive. He held what looked like a cane-knife in one hand, a clutch of flowers and weeds in his other. The weird symbols scribbled on his burlap face appeared to be moving.

He turned to look at Abby, his head leaning to one side.

Abby swallowed hard, took a step back from the window.

'Come on, baby,' Danny called. 'Come back to bed.'

Abby turned to him, scared and confused. She didn't know what the hell was going on, what any of it meant, but she wanted it to end right now.

Danny beckoned her. The knife was still in

his hands. He pointed it at her, traced an X in the air right about where her heart would be. The blade made a palpable scraping sound, like fingernails against a chalkboard. Danny's crude X floated in mid-air, etched into the fabric of her dream. It lingered there momentarily, and then disappeared.

'No,' Abby said. 'I won't let you do this anymore, Danny. You've been haunting me for too long. I want you *out*.'

'Well, come and do something about it, then,' he goaded.

Lori's voice faded in and out. It sounded urgent but Abby still couldn't focus on it, still couldn't tune in.

Abby felt herself drawn towards Danny. Anger burned within her but it seemed to cloud her mind, making it difficult to control her own movements. Danny's energy was too strong.

'That's right,' Danny encouraged. 'Come to Papa.' He wielded the knife, ready to strike.

It felt like wires were attached to Abby's limbs. Like some puppet master was forcing each movement.

Danny was grinning ear to ear. 'You and me have got unfinished business, girl,' he goaded. 'You'll never escape me.' He was still sitting up in bed, the sheets wrapped around his naked body. The wound she'd inflicted on him a year ago was still raw, the bloodied knife gripped tightly in his hand.

Abby suddenly felt very small and frightened. She remembered that feeling from before, from every time he'd struck her in the past, the beatings she'd taken both mentally and physically without question.

Closer, climbing back into bed now.

'That's right,' Danny said. 'You never could resist me, could you?'

It was true. For the last few years of their relationship, Abby had felt trapped, scared. She had dreamed of running, of escaping then just as she did now, but something had kept her locked in, just as she felt locked into this room. Some force had been pulling her strings then just as it did now, and she felt like she couldn't do anything to stop it.

She lay flat on the bed.

Danny traced her body with the knife, as if caressing her. Lust filled his eyes and she thought for an awful moment he was going to rape her. But that wasn't his thing. Violence was his thing. Sex was something he couldn't enjoy, his impotence causing problems in their relationship from a very early stage. The pop psychologist in Abby had often wondered if that was where the manipulation and violence came from. Danny couldn't control his own body, couldn't love her like other men. But he could control *her* body, and while he couldn't make love to her he could sure as hell make a lot of hate.

The blade traced her throat now, Abby waiting for it to slice her skin.

But then she felt her hand move. It reached under the covers, found his small, flat cock and grabbed it with a vice-like grip. Danny didn't expect it. He expected her to lie back and take her dues like she usually would. His eyes popped from his head. His grinning mouth opened, but only a low, winded whine came forth. And then her other hand struck out, pushing against his face. She let go of his cock and he rolled away from her, falling off the bed, taking the covers with him.

Danny struggled to his feet. Stood there cowering, swearing, his face still screwed up. Both hands cradled his groin, his back all hunched over. He threatened all sorts but Abby grabbed the knife once more and rammed it back into that hole in his chest.

He screamed and Abby kept forcing the blade in, realising that she was in control of her body once more, that she was doing all of this on her own, that she could resist him now just as she had resisted him then.

'Now,' a voice said in her head and Abby realized it was Lori's voice.

The panelled door to the room opened and a strong wind blew through. It curled around Danny, seeming to grip him like a fist and pull him towards the door. Yet Abby remained still, as if rooted to the spot. At the last minute Danny reached out with both arms and grabbed onto the doorframe. Holding on with all of his strength, he resisted the invisible force that meant to suck him through the doorway. His eyes were imploring her.

'Please, Abby! You don't wanna do this. We're soulmates, remember? I'm sorry for what I did. You know I never meant to hurt you.'

Abby straightened, suddenly invigorated. Calling on a well of unresolved emotions – all the beatings Danny had given her, the surge of adrenaline she felt the first time she plunged the knife into his chest, the trial, the funny looks, and the people talking behind her back – she cried , 'Well *I* meant to hurt *you*! You hear me you abusive son of a bitch? I enjoyed every last slice of that knife into your rotten flesh and I'd do it all again!'

Danny's expression dropped. His mouth opened as if to say something else and then he was gone, carried by the wind out of Abby's heart and soul and mind.

Her eyes snapped open.

Abby saw Lori, lying on the ground by the campsite. Nanna's burlap man was nowhere to be seen. The book lay opened on the ground nearby, its pages burning as if set alight. Lori's face was strained, her body shaking. It was like she was having some sort of fit.

Abby grabbed her by the shoulders, tried to still her body.

'Lori, snap out of it! It's over!'

Lori's eyes jolted open, immediately wide. It was spooky, like something from an old Dracula movie and Abby found herself pull away.

'Abby?' Lori sat up, looked around. She noticed the book burning beside her, kicked it away with one foot.

Abby embraced her friend.

'Lori, you're okay. Oh, thank God.'

Lori pulled back, studied Abby's face.

'Danny,' she said. 'Is he gone?'

Abby started to cry but a smile filled her face.

'I-I think so,' she whispered. 'I really think so.'

'Oh thank God,' Lori said. 'Because, girlfriend, I could *not* go through that shit again.'

The girls embraced again, gripping each other for what seemed like a very long time, but, in another sense, not long enough.

When they, broke, Abby said, 'There's something else I saw during the vision. Something you should know about. While you were doing your magic, that... *thing* on the porch swing was behind you.'

'Geordi?'

'Whaddayou make of it?'

'Not much really,' Lori said, 'Prolley just your mind working out all the new information. I wouldn't worry about it.'

But something told Abby that Lori *was* worried.

Above the two girls, just out of view, a blood red moon quickly paled.

The night's song continued.

TEN

Abby stood barefoot at the edge of the water. Behind her, at the campsite, the fire's embers continued to glow. Across the lake, oak trees stood side-by-side, tall and draped in a robust green layer that glowed from the light of the moon crouching almost out of view behind them. The dark spaces in between hid all manner of creatures of the night.

The tide washed in and loosened the mud between Abby's toes. The water was colder than she expected. The air was damp and smelled of the sweet after-aroma of rain, a fragrance pretty much unheard of at this time of year in deepest darkest Louisiana.

The others had gone back to bed but Abby dared not sleep and risk missing even one second of this high. And if she *was* asleep, and this was all a dream – as her mind had suggested at one point – then she meant to ride it out to the very end.

Had Lori's cleansing really worked? Was Danny really gone for good? Abby wanted to believe. She imagined life without Danny haunting her thoughts and couldn't help but smile.

Riffing on that thought, Abby crouched, cupped some water into her hands, and let the dark, frigid liquid seep through her fingers. Then she touched her wet hands to her face with the intent of washing away the sleep-deprived sag in her features.

There was a sudden shift in the light, the moon's reflection on the water darkening in color. When Abby lowered her hands she saw that she was not, in fact, alone.

There were eyes on her.

Heart suddenly pumping, Abby squinted, leaned forward for a closer look. *Am I seeing things*? She wasn't wearing her glasses, so it took a moment for her eyes to adjust. As her vision cleared, she could see that there was definitely someone there out on the water, and that someone appeared to be female. Her face was taught and youthful, pale in complexion. She had long, stringy hair that floated away from her face like lazy tentacle-wisps.

There was no sign of movement to suggest

that the girl was treading water, and she was too far out to be standing. At its deepest, Black Water Lake went about forty feet down.

Abby looked away, and back. The girl was gone.

She allowed her gaze to linger there on water. When the girl didn't return, Abby exhaled and dropped her chin to her chest. Suddenly getting some sleep seemed like a good idea. She glanced back at the tent. It looked so small against the backdrop of tree trunks and darkness. So comforting.

The girl was waiting for Abby when she turned back to the lake. Her eyes were closer than before, more intimate. A gasp escaped Abby's lungs. She had to look away rather than bear their weight. She took a few steps back.

'Who are you?' Abby blurted out. 'Whaddayou want?'

The girl didn't respond.

Abby heard rustling behind her and turned sharply.

'Abby? You out there?' a leaden voice called out from the tent.

It was Roxy.

'I'm here,' Abby replied, happy to hear her friend's voice.

'You okay?'

Abby ventured one final look across the lake, but the girl was nowhere to be seen. She turned back to her friend but hesitated before answering her. Could there be a more rational explanation for what she had witnessed than the one she was about to lay on Roxy. The same Roxy who pissed on Lori's 'witchy bullshit' every chance she got. Maybe she was still high. Sure, it had been hours since she had last smoked but Lori's pot was pretty potent. Or was it Lori's cleansing, somehow messing with her head? Abby wasn't ready to venture down that path. She wanted to believe in the cleansing, and whatever mystical mojo went with it. She was afraid of doing anything to ruin it.

'I'm fine,' she told Roxy. 'Think I just need some sleep.'

'You and me both,' Roxy complained. 'Was just about over when I heard you shouting your ass off. What was that about, anyway?'

'Nothing, I was just… singing.' Abby said, smiling weakly. 'Sorry it woke you.'

She climbed inside the tent then zipped the flaps up behind her securely. She could feel Roxy's eyes on her as she slipped into her sleeping bag.

'Damn, girl, you're *weird*,' Roxy muttered.

Abby hoped that was all it was.

ELEVEN

Abby woke with a start and sat up.

She was in the tent, wrapped like a caterpillar in her green sleeping bag.

It was hot. A sweltering Louisiana heat. The morning sun colored the tent's fabric a bright orange. But it wasn't the light that had woken Abby. It was something else…

There it was again: a thud against the side of the tent.

Abby gasped, looked around. She reached beside her, finding an empty sleeping bag. Roxy was gone.

She looked to her other side, finding Lori stirring.

'Hey, what's going on?' Lori said, sleepily, rubbing her eyes.

'Shhhh,' Abby warned, raising a finger to her lips.

Another thud. Both girls jumped this time.

'Jesus, what *is* that?' Lori whispered.

'Someone's throwing stuff at us!' Abby said, still rattled.

Lori blew some air out, exasperated. She slid out of her sleeping bag and bent forward, reaching for the door flaps of the tent.

'What are you doing?' Abby exclaimed.

'Gonna check it out,' Lori said.

'What?! Are you crazy? Stay here!'

'It's probably just Roxy messing around,' Lori said, quickly.

She unzipped the tent flaps, crawled out of the tent.

The trees towered over the clearing, sun bleeding through them. The lake stretched from the point, dark as Hell itself. Lori stepped forward wearing a t-shirt that hung just short of her waist and panties.

'Hello?' she said. 'That you, Rox?'

A thud on the back of her head.

She swung around. On the ground at her feet was an oak nut. Lori rubbed the back of her head.

'Come on,' she said. 'Fun's over, Roxy.'

Disembodied laughter filtered through the

trees.

Lori froze. *What the hell?*

Another pelt, this one hitting her square on the left breast. Lori flinched and let out a tiny yelp. She wasn't wearing a bra and that hurt.

Uproarious applause followed.

Lori wrapped her arms around her chest. Suddenly the culprits and their behaviour seemed thoroughly human and sadly juvenile. Lori frowned and shook her head, storming forward.

'Alright, joke's over,' a voice came from behind.

Lori looked over her shoulder and saw Abby standing outside the tent, clad head-to-toe in her stripy pajamas, adjusting her wireframes and frowning.

More laughter.

Lori turned back to the woods. A man moved out from behind a wide oak stump a few feet in front of her as if pushed forward. He stumbled and fell right at her feet. He was young, good-looking. Kind of preppy. He looked up at Lori, grinning. His head was level with her crotch and Lori glared down at him with one eyebrow raised.

'So, this your idea of hitting on a girl?' she said.

'Guess so,' Preppy said, still on the ground. 'Did it work?'

Lori allowed herself a smile. 'No,' she said.

More laughter from the trees. Another two guys stepped forward.

One looked like a cowboy. He wore a plaid pearl button shirt, with pockets at the front, and a wide-rimmed Stetson. The other seemed a little rougher around the edges, not as clean-cut as his buddies with the sweat-stained wife-beater, long hair and heavy stubble on his face.

'So what are you boys doing out here in the woods, all on your lonesome?' Lori asked.

Preppy pulled himself to his feet. He looked to Lori, then to Abby, running his eyes up and down them both, a wide smile filling his face.

'I was about to ask you girls the very same thing,' he said, then wiped his hand on the leg of his pants and offered it to Lori. 'Where's my manners? My name's Charlie. This here's John C. and that's Jake beside him.'

Roxy returned from her walk to find Lori and Abby sitting by the lake with three guys. They were laughing and joking, everyone in good spirits. One of the guys wore a Stetson.

Roxy rolled her eyes.

'Cozy?' she quipped, setting herself down next to Lori.

She found a cigarette, jammed it between her lips. One of the guys leaned forward, producing a Zippo from his shirt pocket and snapped it alive. Roxy accepted the light, took a heavy drag and then pulled the cigarette from her mouth.

'Thanks,' she said.

'Don't mention it.'

'That's Jake,' John C. said. 'The other one's Charlie. And you know me already.'

'Actually, I'd forgotten you,' Roxy said, flatly. 'Pretty much right after I met you.'

John C. looked hurt.

'Charming,' Charlie said.

'Roxy,' Lori warned, 'Be nice.'

'So, aren't you guys supposed to be hunting or something?' Roxy asked, ignoring her friend. 'Or are we lucky girls today's prey?'

Jake laughed. 'She's cute,' he said. 'I like her.'

'Well, I ain't on the market,' Roxy said. 'So go sniffing somewhere else.'

'*Roxy*!' Lori chided once again. 'Jesus, we're only *talking*.'

Roxy smiled humourlessly. 'And I'm sure that's all you boys have in mind, right?' She winked at John C. 'A nice little chat.'

John C. pulled himself to his feet, quipped, 'Doing just fine until you came along.'

Roxy shot back icy sarcasm, 'Sorry to ruin your evening.'

'Somebody musta really shit in your cornflakes, huh?' John C. snapped, wandering away from the clearing.

Jake followed, laughing.

'A whole bunch of somebodies,' Lori quipped.

Roxy glared at Lori, said, 'You're supposed to be on *my* side.'

'I am,' Lori argued. 'But come on, Roxy. Lighten up. These guys are alright.'

'So far, anyway,' Abby said. She appeared unusually upbeat.

'Hey!' Charlie protested. His manner was playful and Abby smiled in reply.

But Roxy was feeling ambushed, lashing out, 'Is that what the spirits told you, Lori?'

'If you only knew,' Abby smirked. 'Well... not exactly *spirits*, but—'

'Nevermind,' Roxy cut her off. She got up and stormed off in the other direction.

'Roxy,' Abby called after her as she started to get up.

'Let her go,' Lori said. 'She'll cool off eventually.'

'By then it'll be time to go home,' Abby said, pulling herself up and disappearing into the woods after Roxy.

Lori shook her head at all the drama and then stretched out on the grass.

'Well,' Charlie said, fixing her a look. 'I guess it's just you and me, then.'

TWELVE

'Roxy, wait!' Abby called, pulling the other girl's arm.

Roxy stopped, threw her cigarette to the ground, pummelled it with the heel of a cowboy boot. 'How can you act like that after all you said last night?' she fumed. 'I mean... we don't even *know* those guys.'

'What do you mean?' Abby protested.

'All that talk about Danny. What he did to you, how it made you feel. And today, you're fooling around with guys you just met like some horny teenager?!'

'Oh come on,' Abby protested. 'It's not like that!'

'Looked *exactly* like that to me.'

'We're just having fun.'

'The kind of fun I thought you were trying to avoid,' Roxy said. 'You were all over those guys, Abby.'

'Well what if I was?!' Abby chided. 'Jesus, Rox, it's been a while.' She started playing with the daisy bracelet around her arm, picking petals off one flower and throwing them to the ground. 'With Danny, if I even looked at another guy it meant a beating,' she said. 'So, hey, forgive me for actually relaxing for once, and enjoying myself.'

Roxy said nothing, instead dipping her head to the ground.

'It felt *good*, Rox, you know? Acting like a normal girl my age. Talking to boys, having a drink.'

Roxy fixed her a look, said, 'Well that's what worried me. You hear about all kinds in the club I work at. Guys spiking girls' drinks, taking advantage. I just didn't want any of that happening to you, Abby. Especially with all that Danny stuff.'

'Which you don't believe.'

'Which you make hard to believe when I see you acting like that!'

Abby turned away.

Roxy sighed. 'Look, I didn't mean that,' she said.

'You *did* mean it,' Abby countered. 'And you're right to say what you think.'

'No I'm not.'

Abby turned back, fixed Roxy a look. 'Last night, after you went to bed, Lori and I stayed up. She had this book, something about out of body experiences, and she wanted to try something.'

Roxy shook her head, complained, 'More mumbo jumbo.'

But Abby grabbed her by the shoulders, looked into her eyes. 'Well, it worked, Rox! Lori told me to imagine I was back in my old apartment, where it all happened. Then Danny came and together we threw him out. And it really worked – I feel like I'm rid of him for good!'

Roxy went to say something but then stopped herself. She could see in Abby's eyes that she really believed whatever was meant to have happened, that she actually did feel free. And who was Roxy to piss on her parade?

'I don't really know you,' she said instead. 'And I sure as hell know nothing about all that kooky stuff Lori does. But if you feel good, and you're finally free from whatever demons were preying on your mind over the last year,' Roxy allowed herself a faint smile, 'well, that's all that matters, right?'

'Right,' Abby said. 'So let's get back to the others, eh? Have ourselves some fun.'

Roxy rolled her eyes. 'Alright,' she said.

'Come on,' Abby said. 'I'll bet you liked Jake.'

Roxy smiled. 'And I'll bet you'll be wearing a Stetson by the time the day's out.'

Abby laughed giddily.

When they got back to the clearing, there was nobody around. Roxy checked the tent but Lori was nowhere to be seen.

'Where are they?' Abby said.

She looked as worried as Roxy felt.

THIRTEEN

'Shhh,' Lori said, leading Charlie into the barn.

'What do you mean, "Shhh",' Charlie hollered facetiously.

Lori covered his mouth. 'I'm serious,' she said.

Their eyes locked and then they were pulling each other close, kissing passionately.

They stopped for air, looked at each other, a mixture of surprise and lust in both their faces. Lori pulled Charlie deeper into the barn, Charlie dragging the door closed as he went. A dark shadow fell upon them as they made their way to the hay.

'You got any?' Lori asked.

'Any what?' Charlie quizzed.

'You know,' Lori said, reaching for the zipper of his pants.

'Oh, I see…' Charlie said.

The two lovers lay in the hay, sharing a smoke.

'So why're you camping out there in the woods anyway?' Charlie said, then drew hard on the joint.

His skin held a sweaty sheen gained from three rounds of intense sex. His heart was still pumping. The image of Lori's firm tits bouncing as she rode him, of the tight ripple that travelled up from her rounded ass when their hips made contact, of the scrunch-nosed grimace that came over her face when she climaxed, was all still fresh in his mind.

'We were supposed to be staying in the cabin,' Lori told him. 'It's my grandparents' place and they were supposed to be away this weekend, but Gramps took ill. I tried to book a site at the campgrounds but it was full.'

Lori glowed with a similar sheen, lying there next to him, fuck-me hair reaching out like fibrous tentacles, tickling Charlie's shoulder and arm.

'Why didn't you reschedule?'

Lori looked away. 'This weekend's important,' she said. 'My friend Abby went through some shit this time last year and we needed to get her out of the city.'

'Sounds serious,' Charlie said.

'Very serious,' Lori agreed. 'Anyway,' she said, keen to change the subject. 'What brought you guys out here? Roxy mentioned something about hunting?'

'Yep.'

'Hunting what?'

Charlie shrugged. 'Anything that moves, really. Boar, deer, women…' He grinned across at her.

'So, wait,' Lori mocked, 'You're telling me I'm just another mark on your bedpost?'

For a moment, Charlie looked appalled. Then he started to smile. 'Something like that,' he admitted. Then passed the smoke across to Lori.

They lay for a moment, finishing their smoke. The sun was shifting, light piercing through the cracks in the barn's wall, causing Lori to squint.

'Ain't you girls scared camping out there?' Charlie asked.

'Scared of what? The dark?'

'No, the lake. Ain't that Christie Keller territory?'

Lori laughed. 'It ain't me that should be fearin' poor ol' Christie Keller.'

Charlie looked surprised. 'You know the story?'

'Sure, everyone from round these parts does. Nanna don't like to talk about it but Gramps's told me it a few times. Poor ol' Christie, the town witch, being dragged to the lake and drowned. It's a shame, that's for sure. But the way I figure it, me and ol' Christie have too much in common to be afraid of her.'

'What ye mean?'

'Well, we're both half-black, for one.'

'No way!' Charlie said, smiling victoriously as he looked her over anew. 'I would've never guessed.'

'Yep. I could *pass*, as they say.'

'Huh?'

'Back in the old days if you were light-skinned enough – high-yellow, they called it – you could pass for white in order to get a good job or to get in the "whites only" places. Fucked up, huh?'

'But Christie Keller was white,' Charlie argued. 'The story goes that she was born of black parents and—'

'Yeah. And the Earth is flat, too,' Lori quipped. 'We're talking the 1950s. Mixing races could get you killed. Prolley Christie's mom had relations with a white man outside her marriage, or maybe it was forced on her. Who knows. Whatever the case, they didn't want it known. And presto. Instant legend.'

'I never thought about it like that.'

'Most likely she was just really fair. Even more so than I am. People around here can't seem to wrap their heads around that shit, even to this day. It's like the concept of race mixing fries their brains.' Lori made a buzzing sound and pretended to short circuit, laughing afterwards. 'That's why Momma moved me away from here.'

'When did you leave?'

'I was five years old.'

'What about your father?'

'Who?' Lori smiled sadly. 'He was in my mother's life long enough to get her pregnant. No one around here knew him, so people just assumed someone in the church was the father. Then here I come. Being so fair, they saw a white girl, more or less, born to a black woman – just like Christie Keller.'

'You ever wonder about him? Your father, I mean. What traits he passed on to you. I've always been fascinated by that stuff.'

'From what I hear he was as redneck as they come. Woulda given your John C. Lane a run for his money. As far as traits… I guess I got his color and Momma's looks – thank God.'

'Thank God you're not dark-skinned?'

'Nooo!' Lori said. 'God no! I'm *proud* of my black heritage. Why you got a problem with that?'

'Not at all,' Charlie said. 'Especially when it comes in such a pretty package.'

Lori chaffed.

Charlie threw his hands up and said, 'Whoa!

Hold on now! I didn't mean anything by— I was only trying to—'

'Relax.' Lori said. 'I shouldn't have come at you like that. You were only trying to be nice.' She looked at Charlie with puppy-dog eyes, planted her opened palm on his chest, and slid her fingers downward tracing the contour of his firm, young body. 'You forgive me?' she cooed.

'Well, since you put it like that…' Charlie quipped.

They started to make out.

It felt nice to lie there. As close to perfect as could be, in a romanticized, Lifetime Channel sort of way. Lori was on her back. Charlie on his side fondling her hair and devouring her with his eyes. He caressed her face with the back of his hand, moving on to her breasts, down her stomach, and—

Lori shifted, turning her hip away from him.

Charlie pulled his hand back, asked, 'What's wrong?'

'Nothing,' she said. 'Just thinking how long we've been away. Maybe we should get back to the others.'

Lori pulled herself up.

Charlie grabbed her arm.

She startled, turned to face him.

He held her eyes. 'You're not just another mark,' he said.

'What?'

'You know, what you said earlier about being a mark on the bedpost? That's not how I see you.'

Lori smiled, bent down to kiss Charlie.

'Come on,' she said. 'The others will be worried.'

As Charlie stood up and brushed himself down, they heard the door pull open.

A breeze pushed through the opened barn door and kicked up hay. Lori grabbed Charlie by the arm and pulled him behind a support beam. They huddled together, Lori stealing a glance at the doorway.

'Who *is* it?' Charlie whispered.

Lori shushed him and—

The snout of a shotgun crept through the gap in the door, a heavy work boot following. She couldn't see the face, but Lori already knew who was coming through.

'It's Gramps!' she whispered, dragging Charlie towards the back wall of the barn.

'What?' Charlie protested. 'I thought you said he was under the weather.'

'Well, not anymore,' Lori said.

'Who's there?!' a familiar voice rang out, the old black man shimmying into the barn, eyes wrapped in shades. 'I may be blind but I ain't deaf. And I can sniff you out!'

Charlie went to laugh but Lori covered his mouth. 'He'll shoot if he hears us,' she warned.

Gramps heard something, waved the shotgun threateningly.

Lori pointed at a ladder.

They climbed up the ladder onto the barn's loft, Charlie taking the lead, Lori following. They crept across the hay-peppered floor towards the front porch of the barn then let themselves down the outside ladder.

They hit the ground running. The ground

felt hard and baked on their bare feet. Lori went one way – toward the main path, back towards the car – but Charlie had started down another track.

'This way,' he called.

Lori stopped, made a face at him. *What*?!

'It's a short-cut back to your campsite,' he said.

Lori hesitated, remembering that she meant to retrieve a flashlight from her car, but it was parked in the clearing back down the other track.

The barn door creaked, and then pushed open.

Fuck it, she thought and followed Charlie into the woods.

FOURTEEN

Roxy and Abby followed the river, tracing its flow away from the lake to find the campsite that John C. had mentioned. Roxy was starting to get worried. It wasn't like Lori to take off like this. Sure, she was flighty and easily wowed, but she wasn't stupid enough to just shoot through without telling anyone.

And then there was all that mystical bullshit…

Roxy recalled that weird vibe she'd felt last night as she stood by the car, smoking. She wasn't *fully* ready to accept Lori's mumbo jumbo, but would have to admit to there being something different in the air. Maybe Mother

Nature, or whatever you wanted to call it, did have a presence you could feel inside you. Especially around this weirdass place.

The two girls walked in silence. They reached the guys' camp a little further upstream but found none of them there, so they backtracked their way along the lake.

It was getting hotter, the sun burning high in the sky, taking its toll.

'I don't trust those guys,' Roxy griped, running a hand through her hair.

'Seems like you don't trust guys, period,' Abby said.

'Why should I? They only want one thing,' Roxy said. 'Well, two things, actually – pussy and money – and they'll say or do whatever it takes to get them.'

Abby shook her head. 'They're not all like the ones you deal with at the strip club.'

Roxy laughed. 'Here we go.'

'What?'

'You gonna start judging me now?'

'*No!* Geez, Roxy. Why do you always hafta get so defensive? I was just making an observation is all.'

Roxy stopped walking and pushed air out of her lungs. She looked over at Abby, caught a doe-eyed look and suddenly her anger gave way to guilt. Verbal sparring was par for the course with the girls back at the club. But Abby was that type of "good girl" that Roxy both envied and pitied.

'Okay, I'm sorry, Abby,' she said. 'You're the last person I should be yelling at.'

'It's okay.'

'No. It's not okay. Yell at me. Call me a bitch. Something. I mean… don't you ever get mad?'

'Yeah… and look what happened,' she replied.

'You mean Danny?' Roxy said. 'Girl, you gotta stop beating yourself up for doing what you had to do. If you hadn't it would've been you laying six feet under.'

Abby looked at her feet.

'Ok. Maybe that was the wrong choice of words,' Roxy added.

'I know what you're saying,' Abby began, 'It's just that—'

'Look, Abby, I like you,' Roxy cut in. 'You seem like a pretty cool chick. But you're way too nice. I'm not saying you have to be like me or anything but you've gotta learn to put your foot down. Stand up for yourself. Don't be afraid to be a bitch sometimes.'

'That's just not me, though.'

Roxy walked up, slung her arm over Abby's shoulders, and pulled her close.

'Tell you what. I'm gonna make it a point over the next couple of days to help you find your inner bitch. Deal?'

'Deal,' Abby replied with a crinkle-nosed smile that made Roxy want to squeeze her harder.

They continued walking, passing a line of shrubs nestled at the feet of the oak trees. The hot, humid air simmered between their lattice of arthritic looking branches.

Abby stopped for a moment, wiped the sweat from her brow.

'Why don't we check the cabin?' she said.

'Maybe Lori went to check in on her folks. Plus, I have to use the bathroom. '

'Just pee in the bushes, girl,' Roxy laughed. 'I'll stand watch.' Abby tossed Roxy a look. Seemed like their bonding hadn't reached that level. 'Okay, come on,' Roxy said. 'We'll head back to the cabin, then.'

Which suited her fine. Truth was, Roxy had just about had all the footfall her Cowboy boots could take. She felt sweaty, would have killed for a shower. And a swig of beer wouldn't go amiss.

They followed the path back round towards the cabin, arriving at the clearing where the car was parked.

Abby was the first to see it, stopping dead in her tracks and throwing one hand to her mouth.

Roxy had been lighting a cigarette when she noticed Abby stopping. She looked up to see what was the matter now and the cigarette immediately dropped out of her hands.

'Holy fuck,' she said.

FIFTEEN

'Some short-cut,' Lori complained as she pushed forward swatting aside thorny branches and high-stepping over tangled vines. 'You call this a trail?'

Charlie was a few feet in front of her, moving deftly through the brush. 'It's there. You just have to know where to look,' he said pulling and stomping and kicking out a path for Lori. 'Just follow my lead.'

'If I didn't know any better I'd think you were fixin' to kidnap me or something,' Lori joked.

'Can't believe you'd think that of me,' Charlie protested. 'I'm the nice guy of the group.' He made finger quotes. '*College Boy*.'

'Is that what they call you?' Lori sniggered.

'Yep. But they're only jealous cos I get the girls.'

He winked and Lori rolled her eyes.

'So, the old man,' he said. '"Gramps" or whatever you call him. He really blind?'

'Sure is.'

'Tha hell's he doing walking around with a shotgun for?'

'Just cos his eyes don't work doesn't mean he can't see.'

'What?' Charlie said, his face twisting.

Lori could have explained how Gramps' remaining senses had been enhanced via an old incantation that Nanna cooked up on her stove. She could have told him that she was a witch and Nanna and Gramps practiced Voodoo as far back as she could remember. But today... this weekend... however long this thing with College Boy here lasted, Lori just wanted to be Lori, the exotic-looking, mixed race chick. 'It means he's got a nose like a bloodhound and ears like a bat,' she explained.

'Yeah. That's cool and all, but you really should take that thing away from him before somebody gets hurt.'

Lori shrugged.

'And what about that pouch round his neck? Is that something magical and all?'

Here we go, Lori thought. 'It's called a grigri bag,' she said half-heartedly. 'It's worn for protection. Sort of like wearing a crucifix.'

'Protection from what?' Charlie frowned.

Lori thought for a moment. A sly grin melted to the surface. 'From horny white boys,' she said.

Charlie laughed. 'I'm the one who needs protection with all the weird ass shit going on in your family. I say or do the wrong thing and your folks'll turn me into a toad or something.'

Lori smirked and then changed the subject. 'So, whadda you gonna tell your friends when they ask you what happened?'

Charlie seemed blindsided by the question. He thought for a second, and said in a mischievous tone, 'I'll tell 'em we went for a hay-ride.'

'You're bad,' Lori scolded, laughing as she spoke.

They pushed through another nestle of branches to spot a clearing up ahead.

'This opens up to the main trail,' Charlie told Lori. 'From there it leads right to your campsite so—'

Something moved in the bushes on the right. Something big. Lori slapped her hand over her chest and yelped.

She looked at Charlie, whispered, 'Probably just the wind, right?'

Charlie pressed one finger across his lips.

He was eagle-eyeing a tangle of shrubs surrounding an oddly protruding tree-stump. The movement had come from there.

Charlie slinked forward, cat-like.

The shrubs rustled again, violently this time. Charlie froze.

Lori startled again and said, 'That's definitely too big to be a—'

'SHHHHHH!'

Something dark and furry shot out of tangle of shrubs and thumped against a tree opposite. Heavy hands or paws slapped against wood. Claws scratched and skittered, moving upward. They sounded sharp. The skitter-scratching stopped mid-way between the ground and the first tier of branches, which was just about head-level with Charlie. He searched the ground and picked up an arm-long stick. Held it like a baseball bat and approached the oak tree on creep.

'Are you serious?' Lori protested.

'Just hang on,' Charlie shooed. 'I'm guessin' it's a coon. Jake's been trying to bag one since we got here. He'll be SO pissed...'

Lori could never kill another living thing – except maybe for a roach – and she had no interest in witnessing it first hand. Especially by means of a slow, tortuous bludgeoning. No way.

'Charlie, wait,' she said.

But Charlie wasn't listening. Raising one hand to Lori, he picked up a rock with the other and flung it to his right. Then he moved left at a slight arc, to the front of the oak.

Lori followed, finding a bigass raccoon clinging motionless to the tree trunk, staring off in the direction of the rock.

She watched Charlie crank the stick back, making eyes at the animal's bulk. She needed to do something to stop him.

'Pssst,' she called.

He glanced back at her, angrily, but then his face softened. Lori had her shirt hiked up, exposing her breasts. 'You do it and you won't see these ever again,' she mouthed.

Charlie blew out some air and then with a smirk on his face, shook his head at Lori's ultimatum. He turned back to the raccoon, unfocused, erect, and…

A 12" Gurkha knife sliced through the air and impaled the large rodent to the tree through the back of the head. Charlie jumped back and fell on his ass. The stick flew out of his hand. The raccoon let out a terrible shriek, flexed its limbs, and then fell to a limp dangle from the crooked blade.

'Son of a bitch!' Charlie spat, picking himself up off of the ground. 'How bout a warning next time, ya dipshit!'

The woods seemed to laugh at him, but it was only Jake and John C. Lane seeping out from where the thicket spread between two oaks, strung together by vines.

'Calm down, College Boy,' Jake said as he walked up and pulled the knife with the dead raccoon stuck to it from the tree. Smiling at his prize, he grabbed a clutch of the animal's fur. 'That wasn't nowhere near you.'

Lori winced at the sound as Jake tore the knife from the dead coon's flesh.

John C. helped wipe the dirt from Charlie's back and then gave his friend an affectionate pat on the shoulder. 'You'd think he saw fucking Bigfoot the way he took off after that thing.'

'Damn straight,' Jake agreed. 'You boys'll be singing a different tune once you taste my momma's coon pot pie.'

Jake wiped the blade on the dead animal's fur and then slid the knife back into the crooked sheath strapped to his thigh. He glanced over at Charlie's stick, and dismissed it with a smile. 'Most you'da done with that is piss it off,' he said, walking back toward the thicket that spat him out.

Charlie silently mimicked Jake to his back. It made Lori smile.

John C's eyes narrowed as he watched the couple. 'So... what've *you two* been up to?' he asked, smiling lasciviously.

'Wouldn't you like to know,' Charlie said. He went to pull Lori close.

'Get away from her,' a voice came from nearby.

Lori watched helplessly as Roxy appeared from the woods, swinging a branch to connect with Charlie's jaw, sending him sprawling across the dry ground. 'Jesus!' she cried.

Roxy was lining up to strike again but Abby grabbed her, held her back.

The other two guys ran to the aid of their friend.

Lori was beside them now. 'What's wrong with you?' she shouted at Roxy. 'Christ, you could have killed him!'

She went to help Charlie but John C. stepped up to her. 'Get away from him,' he said firmly.

'Look, I'm sorry,' Lori said, looking down at a dazed Charlie. 'I don't know what got into her.'

'Shut up, Lori,' Roxy said, pulling roughly away from Abby. 'I can speak for myself.'

She looked to John C.

'You bastard,' she spat. She caught a glimpse of Jake's hands and the bloody towel pressed between them, and said to John C. 'What? You weren't man enough to do it yourself?'

'Hey. I ain't got nothing to do with... whatever this is,' Jake said weakly.

'What the hell's wrong with you?' Charlie said, one hand dabbing blood from his bust lip.

'Bitch is insane,' John C. muttered.

'I'll tell you what's insane,' Roxy countered. 'That mess you made back *there*.' She pointed.

'What?' Lori stepped forward. 'What do you mean, *mess*?'

'Tell her,' Roxy ordered.

John C. and Jake looked at each other, confused.

'Tell her *what*?' John C. asked.

'Tell her what you guys did,' Roxy pressed, her voice shaking with anger. She patted her left palm with the stick. 'GO ON, TELL HER!'

Jake stiffened up. 'Look, I don't care how pretty you are, you're not gonna—'

'Lady,' John C. interrupted, hands raised, palms pressed forwards, 'I don't know what the hell you're talking about and I'm sure Jake and Charlie don't either.'

Roxy pointed at John C. 'I saw you last night, remember? Down by the car. Then I get there ten minutes ago and the damn thing's trashed.'

'What?!' John C. said. 'And you think we did it?!'

'I frickin' saw you,' Roxy persisted. 'Plus,

look at his hands,' she said aiming her eyes at Jake.'

Jake bristled at Roxy's accusatory glare and shot back a look that said, *'Yeah. So.'*

'He just killed a friggin' raccoon,' John C. said pointing at the ground near Jake's feet where the dead animal lay on its side next to an old cracked leather satchel, and a camo-colored canteen.

Jake slid his foot away to give Roxy a clear view.

Roxy made a face at the dead thing and then said, 'That doesn't prove a thing!'

'Okay, let's all calm down,' Lori jumped in.

'No. Lori. You ain't seen what they did. They were all in on it. I know they were.'

'Jesus, Mary and Joseph,' John C. whined, exasperated.

Lori looked to Roxy, said, 'What's wrong with the car?'

Roxy divided her glare between the three guys, lingering on John C., whom she assumed was the mastermind behind the whole thing. 'I'll show you,' she said. 'But I want them to come too.'

SIXTEEN

They stood around the car like dumbstruck kids. Only Lori was moving, fussing around the little thing like a grieving mother. Its tires were slashed. Every bit of glass, save the windshield, was smashed. The bodywork was ruined:

scratched, scraped, dented, its flowers wilted and its go-faster stripes quelled. Someone had gone to town on the little car and left it in real bad shape.

But that wasn't the worst of it.

Written on the windshield, in what looked like blood, were the words 'NO ESCAPE'.

Roxy glared at the guys. 'Wanna explain yourselves?' she said.

But their faces looked every bit as shocked as the girls'. 'You really think we did this?' John C. said, finally.

'Your hands,' Roxy said to Jake, pointing at the words scribbled on the car. 'That looks like blood to me.'

'John C. told you already how I only just killed that coon,' Jake said. 'Now how the hell would I, or any of us, have time to hike up here from where we were and do all this? Explain that to me.'

The other two guys nodded, mumbling agreement.

Roxy didn't have an answer. Feeling ambushed, she looked to the other two girls.

Lori was still fussing over the car.

Abby was standing back from the rest of the pack. Her face was chalk-white. Even in the clearing's light, she looked like death. Her eyes glistened, as if damp. She raised one hand to her mouth.

A sudden cry from Lori pulled Roxy away from Abby. Lori suddenly ran to Roxy, curling into her friend's embrace.

'Is this what you wanted?' Roxy said to John C. 'See the upset you've caused?'

The redneck was riled. He went for Roxy but the two other boys held him back. 'You're out of line, lady,' he sneered, pointing at her. '*Way* out of line!'

'Why'd you do it?' Roxy pushed. 'Because I shot you down last night. Because I wouldn't fuck you? Is that it?!'

John C. was seething now. 'I swear, I'm gonna—'

Another voice interrupted him. 'Oh look at this mess!' Roxy turned to see Nanna running towards them. 'Who would do such a thing?'

'Nanna!' Lori cried, peeling herself from Roxy, allowing herself to be swallowed up by the old black woman's considerable bosom.

'There there, child,' Nanna soothed. 'There there…'

The old woman eyed up all those gathered as she comforted Lori.

'It's *him*,' Abby said, shaking her head. '*He* did this.'

'That's what I said,' Roxy agreed. 'Fucker can't take getting shot down.'

'No,' Abby said. 'Not *him*.' She looked at John C. like he was nothing but a nuisance, a distraction. 'I recognise that writing. And those words.' She shook her head. 'It's what he would tell me when I talked of running out on him. "There's no escaping me, babe," he'd say. "I'll come after you."'

'What are you talking about?' Roxy asked.

'Danny,' Abby said. She looked up, tears streaming down her cheeks. 'Danny did this.'

***

'Okay,' So let's get some perspective on all of this,' Roxy said. 'Danny's dead, sweetheart. It couldn't be him. But *that* fucker and his lackies,' Roxy pointed once more at John C., 'are very much alive. And *he* was here last night. Tried his best to get into my pants, but I shot him down and he weren't too happy about that. This morning, the car's wrecked with some animal's blood all over it. Grizzly Adams over there's got blood on his hands. This case couldn't be more open and shut.'

'Hot *and* funny,' Jake quipped to John C. 'Better hold on to this one.'

'So this is all some big joke to you?' Roxy seethed.

'Yer the one with the jokes,' Jake countered.

'You're a fucking joke.'

Jake smirked at Roxy's juvenile retort.

'You know, you're a real piece-a-work,' John C. said.

'You sure thought so last night.'

John C. rolled his eyes and threw his hands up in surrender. 'I give up,' he said and turned away from her.

'You can't just walk away,' Roxy yelled.

'Would you please, for the love of God, shut your mouth?'

'Come and make me, boy,' Roxy countered. And she meant it. She'd met his type before. The club was full of them, guys who were all talk and little action. She wasn't frightened of them and she wasn't frightened of this prick.

Nanna spoke next. 'Pray, child,' she said, her deep brown eyes firmly fixed on Abby, while

Lori still burrowed into her sizeable breasts, 'what makes you think a dead man did this?'

'I ain't felt right since coming here,' Abby said. 'Y'all know that. It's like Danny's been inside me all along. And since I got here, his grip's felt tighter.'

'Who's this Danny?' Nanna asked.

Roxy sighed. 'It's her no-good ex-boyfriend. Bastard beat the shit out of her but she got him in the end. Put the son-of-a-bitch down like the woman-beatin' sewer rat he was.' Roxy made sure to find Abby's eyes as she said that last bit.

'Mind your language now, girl,' Nanna warned.

'Sorry. It's just—'

'I don't care what it is,' Nanna said. 'A lady doesn't use that kind of language.'

Roxy sighed. 'Yes ma'am.'

Nanna nodded acceptance and then turned back to Abby. 'So, you think this dead ex-boyfriend is haunting you somehow?' she asked.

'No,' Roxy said. 'There's no mumbo-jumbo going on.' She pointed once again at John C. '*Him* and his two cronies did this.'

'Hush now!' Nanna chided Roxy and then, looking back to Abby, said, 'Come on, child, out with it.'

'Lori tried to help with some meditation or something and it *seemed* to work,' Abby began, sniffing back some tears. 'Something lifted. I felt free again, good for the first time in a year. I thought he was gone. But this…' Her face screwed up and her body started shaking as she stared at the words written in blood on the car's windshield. 'I think he did this, I really do.

And I know it doesn't make sense, I know he's dead, but this is Danny's work. I'm sure of it!'

'Oh for Christ's sake,' Roxy started but Nanna raised her hand, stopping her.

'Stranger things have happened,' the old woman said. 'Black Water's known for malevolent forces.'

'It's just water. And some gaddam woods,' Roxy said. 'And that's a car. And *that prick* over there—'

'Now, I told you about that language, young lady,' Nanna broke in. 'I don't care how you talk around your friends, but I'm not gonna stand for that kind of language in my presence. You understand me?!'

It took everything for Roxy to stifle her emotions, but she did just that, sheepishly nodding at the old woman's retort.

Nanna continued, 'That water has witnessed a lot over the years, and I've every fear it could twist a person, pull something evil from them.' She patted Lori's back as she talked, like she was a child that needed winding. 'The long arm of the law hasn't always stretched round these parts and people have abused that privilege. If a man died of unnatural causes, this was the best place to dump him. And then there was young Christie Keller...'

'Oh you have got to be kidding me,' Roxy said to Nanna, throwing her hands in the air. 'I thought you said the campground was behind all that.'

'I said that I *suspect* they're behind these recent sightings. Dan't mean there ain't something foul here in these woods.'

Roxy thrust a finger at John C, said, 'Yeah. And he's standing right there.'

'You're crazy,' John C scoffed.

'Oh! *I'm* the crazy one?'

'Lori told us about Christie Keller last night,' Abby cut in, her face white like a sheet. 'She's that witch, right?'

'Yeah, she was a witch alright,' John C. said, seemingly glad not to be the centre of attention for once. 'And they drowned her at the lake for her sins. Everyone knows that story.'

Nanna smiled sadly. 'Christie was a strange girl alright, there ain't nobody can deny that. But she weren't no witch.'

'Okay, I've heard enough,' Roxy said. 'I've had my fill of witches and Voodoo and ghosts. Next you'll be telling me the Loch Ness Monster did that to the car. I think it's time to put a little real world spin on this.' She looked at John C., her eyes narrowing. 'I say we get the cops up here, let them get to the bottom of all of this.'

SEVENTEEN

Roxy looked at Nanna. 'You've got a phone in the cabin, right?'

'You really are a disrespectful somethin', aren't you?' the old woman replied.

'Look,' Roxy said, pointing at the three guys. 'It was *them*. I know it was.'

'Now wait a minute,' Charlie said. 'Let's just think about this for a second—'

'What's there to think about?' Roxy cut in. 'If y'all are *really* innocent, like you say, you won't mind the cops dusting the car and printing you. Right?'

Charlie rubbed his mouth. 'Look,' he began with a placating smile, 'it's nothing to do with the car. It's just that it ain't *exactly* legal to be hunting around these parts. Not since they opened the Stogies.'

'That a fact,' Roxy said, feigning interest. She looked to Nanna, played nice, 'May I *please* use your phone?'

'Now come on,' Charlie said, more serious now. He ruffled in his pocket, pulled his wallet out. It was one of those big black leather ones that businessmen would carry around. Roxy had seen them at the club. *Probably his daddy's*, she mused. 'We can pay for the damage, clear this thing up.' He clicked open the wallet. 'What'll it take? Two, three hundred dollars?'

'Oh, you want a value on this?' Roxy mocked. 'The heartache and upset that you jerkoffs caused?' She stroked her chin with several painted fingers, pretended to think for a while. 'I'd say spending some quality time in jail should suit y'all just fine. Harassment and criminal damage charges oughta see to that.'

Charlie was momentarily numb, standing there, his wallet dangling limp from his hand.

John C. stepped forward and said, 'Maybe it was somebody from the Stogie's did all this. You ever figure that?'

'Oh please,' Roxy scoffed. 'What? They hiked five miles downstream just to randomly vandalize somebody's car? It was you and your friends and you know it.'

'SHUT UP!' John C. suddenly screamed. 'We didn't do it! Can't you get that through your thick, *whorin'* skull?!'

'Now hold on a minute,' Nanna scolded John C. 'What I said to her goes double for you bein' that she's a lady. What is it with you young' uns? In my day a man would never speak to a woman in such-a-way.'

'That's because she was completely sub-servient to his ass,' Roxy muttered under her breath.

Nanna turned and looked at Roxy. 'And women didn't use such vulgar language,' she chided again. 'Now, go on. There's a phone in the cabin. Why don't you call the law, like you said.'

Roxy's face lit up. She started off toward the cabin. She made it about fifteen feet and then turned. 'What's the number?'

'Five eight two...' Nanna tried. 'Oh, I've for-gotten the next bit.' She thought about it for a while, eyes closed. 'Just go on. It'll come to me in a minute.'

Roxy sighed, waited.

'What about us?' John C. asked the old woman. 'The cops are gonna have something to say about us huntin' round here.'

'Oh, I wouldn't worry about Sheriff Taylor,' Nanna assured.

'Why not?'

'Cos Sam Taylor is a drunk and a fool who don't do his job properly. Most he'll do is give you boys a tongue-lashing over the huntin' – *if* he even comes up here at all.'

'Oh that's just great,' Roxy laughed.

'We didn't do this, you know,' John C. stepped forward and said to the old woman.

The other guys nodded.

'Oh! *Okay*! Then who did?' Roxy challenged.

Nanna threw her a side-eyed glance. She was about to rebuke her yet again when Abby said, 'I told you who it was, Roxy. It was Danny.'

Roxy sucked her teeth, her face going bright red. 'Gimme a fucking break,' she said under her breath as she turned around and found herself face-to-face with Nanna. In the time it took for Roxy to gasp, the old woman cocked her meaty arm back to last year and gave Roxy an open-handed smack that spun her a full quarter turn to the right.

Roxy cried out in pain and threw her hand over her left cheek. She whipped her head toward Nanna, ready to spit venom, but there was no one there. She spun around to confused looks from Lori, Abby, and the others standing around the demolished car. Nanna was there with them, where she had been the entire time, it seemed.

Roxy's temper melted, replaced by the same expression the others had.

'You alright?' Charlie said.

The left side of her face was still on fire and throbbing.

'Yeah,' Roxy said. 'Just fine.'

Her eyes found Nanna. There was a knowing glint in the old woman's gaze.

Roxy took a few steps backward, turned, and continued up to the cabin. She looked back at the group, zeroing in on Nanna, but the old black woman just raised an eyebrow.

Roxy kept walking.

EIGHTEEN

'But it felt so real,' Roxy kept telling herself as she tried to wrap her mind around the bitch-slap of the century.

Rather than accept it as some kooky Voo-doo shit, Roxy searched for a more pragmatic solution as she made her way toward the cabin. She'd caught half of some show on TV recently going on about the brain and its ability to produce vivid hallucinations under stress and, hell, she'd let herself get pretty worked up back there.

And then there was the pot. Sure, she'd got it from Lori but who did Lori get it from? Maybe it'd been laced. Roxy once worked with a girl who almost lost her mind from a joint laced with PCP.

Maybe that would explain Abby getting all paranoid, thinking that Danny, her dead boy-friend, had wrecked the car. Then again, Lori seemed fine and she'd probably had the most.

Roxy reached the porch, eyes clamping on Geordi the burlap man. She'd almost forgotten his crazy ass but there he was, propped up like some old scarecrow, creepy as all hell. Roxy thought about going around back so she didn't have to walk past the damn thing, but the rebel in her said otherwise. She cleared the porch steps in one bound and, without looking at him, stuck up her middle finger at Geordi on her way in the door.

Gramps stood in the living area as Roxy came through. His face was creased in concern.

'Who's that?' he asked. 'Who's just come in?'

'Roxy. Lori's friend.'

The old man sniffed, light bouncing off his sunglasses as he moved his head around deciphering the smell of her perfume. 'What's happening out there, girl?' he asked. 'All I hear is shoutin' and cryin'. Yet nobody thinks to tell old Gramps anything bout it.'

'Some redneck's banged up Lori's car real good,' Roxy said. She found the phone on the nearby wall, lifted the receiver. 'I'm calling the cops.' She spun the dialler ringing out the numbers Nanna had told her... and then a few more. As she held the receiver to her ear, Roxy remembered that Nanna had never finished giving her the number, yet she had dialled something pretty much as if it was second nature to her and now it was ringing on the other end.

How did I do that? she mused.

'What?' Gramps said, pulling Roxy out of her thoughts. 'Who hurt Lori? And don't be calling no cops. Sheriff Sam Taylor is a useless sum-bitch.'

'Nobody *hurt* her,' Roxy said. 'At least not yet. And I *am* calling the cops.'

She heard a grumble from the old man, watched him fumble about in the kitchen area. He found an old trunk in the corner, felt around its edges for a catch. He pulled the trunk open, lifted a shotgun into his hands. He stooped once again, feeling around the trunk for some rounds. He unclicked each barrel, loaded them, then snapped it shut, ready to do business.

Roxy's call connected, a voice answering. She started talking down the phone, laying out the story.

Gramps sniffed the air again then, using his free hand, found the door and wandered on out, gun pointing forward.

Roxy watched him go without a word.

The phone kept ringing.

Sheriff Sam Taylor lounged back in his office chair as the phone continued to ring.

In his hands was an envelope. He'd opened it and laid the contents out on the desk in front of him, one hand feeling around in his desk drawer for his glasses.

Once on, he studied the letter again to see if there was anything he'd missed from reading it without his glasses. But there wasn't. Whitney was looking for a divorce. The hearing was planned for two weeks' time.

'D.I.V.O.R.C.E.' Dolly Parton had once sang and her words were ringing through Sam's head. He found himself humming as he read the letter for the third time.

He rolled his wedding ring around his special finger. That's what Whitney had called it when they got engaged: 'You got me a ring for my special finger,' she'd said.

Well not so special now, Sam thought.

The phone kept ringing, unanswered.

There was a tut from the desk opposite, Sam's PA, Edna Burns, reaching for her phone.

'Well I'll just get that for you, Sheriff, shall I?' She lifted the receiver said, 'Sheriff's office' in a tone no more enthusiastic, then listened.

Sam folded the letter, set it at the other side of his desk in the tray marked IN.

He looked across the office, raised his eyebrows as Edna jotted down some notes, receiver still fixed to her ear. 'Another sighting?' he whispered, expecting the latest bullshit tale about Christie Keller.

Edna shook her head, placed one hand over the receiver. 'Vandalism. Paint job done on a car.'

An actual crime. Sam didn't expect to hear that and his face said as much. 'At the Stogies?'

'The Sawyer place.'

Sam waved his hand. It was a well used gesture that meant, *No. Not right now. Take a message.*

Edna sighed, took some details.

Sam stood up from his desk, reached for his car keys. *Going out*, he mouthed over to Edna. Which really meant, *You hold the fort. I won't be back today.*

Edna frowned again in that way she did but Sam ignored it. He wasn't in the mood today and, hell, being the sheriff of a town like this meant a certain amount of making your own rules and suiting your damn self.

He left the office. Headed right across the road to Tom's Bar.

Tom was in as always, shooting the shit with the Saturday afternoon crowd. He nodded as Sam Taylor entered, dipping into the cooler to retrieve him a bottle of Bud.

'Sheriff,' he said, cracking the beer open and passing it to Taylor.

'Tom.' Sam filed into a seat by the bar, lifted the beer and took a swig. He nodded at the man beside him; an old farm hand named Fred Redmond. Fred nodded back, sipped his own beer.

'All quiet on the western front?' Tom asked.

'Just how we like it,' Sam replied.

Tom smiled, fetched himself a whisky and downed it quickly. It was the kind of movement you'd miss, it was done so fluidly.

'I notice Doc Jamison's finally handing the towel in,' Tom said. 'Who'd have thought it, eh?'

Sam nodded. 'Guess everyone's got to quit some time. But that old engine just kept going. What is he, eighty-five, eighty-six?'

'Eighty-seven,' Tom said. 'We had his birthday bash in the bar here last March.'

'I remember that,' Sam said. 'Geez, the doc's that old? Hell of a man for it.'

'Damn straight.'

Sam took another swig from his Bud, brought the bottle down. 'Whitney wrote,' he said, playing with his wedding ring again.

'Did she, now?'

'Wants a divorce.'

'Like the Dolly Parton s—'

'Damn it, Tom, that song's been rattling through my head since I read her lawyer's letter.'

'Give it to her, Sam.'

The chief fixed the barman a cool stare.

'Seriously, let her go.'

'She's already gone, Tom. This just means she ain't coming back.'

'Well she ain't. And you shouldn't want her back.'

Sam Taylor said nothing for a second. Looked down at his drink, pushed it aside. He started spinning the ring on his 'special' finger again and in a quiet voice said, 'I ain't innocent in all of this, you know.'

Tom sighed. Placed a hand on his old friend's shoulder and looked him straight in the eye. 'You can't punish yourself forever, Sam,' he said. 'You made a few mistakes. What man hasn't? Hell, you've done a lot of good in this town to make up for it.'

'I'm the sheriff, Tom. People should be able to look up to me.'

'And they do, Sam.'

'Do they? You know how many people goad me when I go to as much as hand out a speed-ing ticket. Every day, Tom! Every damn day I get it!'

Sam didn't realize he was shouting until he looked around. The afternoon drinkers looked back at him, bemused. Someone lifted their drink from the bar and carried it to a table. The guys shooting pool downed their beers and left instead of racking up another game.

'You got to keep your cool, Sam,' Tom said. 'This is your business, nobody else's. Don't want it getting around town now, do you?'

Sam laughed. 'Too late. I'll bet it's already around town,' he said. 'Like everything else.'

'Let me guess: Edna?'

'Letter came to the office. Edna opened it along with all the other mail and you can be damn sure she read it too.'

Tom shook his head. 'She's some dame...'

'She's that alright,' Sam agreed before sinking the rest of his Bud.

Tom took the empty bottle, set his friend up with another. He fetched himself another shot of whiskey and downed it quickly, dumped the drained glass into the sink under the bar.

'There's been talk in the bar about Whitney,' he said gingerly. 'About who she's been seen with.'

Sam raised his eyes

'You know that lawn guy you hired?'

'What?' Sam laughed. 'Don't be stupid, that guy's just a kid.'

'I know, Sam' Tom said. He looked around the bar, lowered his voice. 'But that's what folks have been saying.'

Sam shook his head. Then his smile faded as he seemed to entertain the idea. 'Why didn't you tell me before now?'

'Cos I know what you're like when you get a drink and a wild idea into your head, that's why.'

Sam looked away.

'Sign the papers, Sheriff,' Tom said, 'Give her what she wants and move on.'

He left Sam, went to serve another customer.

Sam smiled and took a swig of his new beer. *What she wants is the problem*, he mused.

NINETEEN

The old man trundled into the clearing with resolve, sniffing the air like a dog on a scent and moving remarkably well for his age. The gun was aimed squarely in front of him, as he came. Pretty much everyone gathered by the car watched his descent.

It was Lori that spoke first. 'Gramps,' she said, walking slowly towards him, her arms outstretched. 'It's okay. Nobody's hurt.'

'Who done what to your car, child?' the old man barked.

'Nobody, Gramps. Now, please...'

'Well, *somebody* did,' Nanna corrected before raising her voice so the old man was sure to hear, then adding, 'But it ain't nothing for you to worry about. So put that shotgun down and let's wait and see what the law has to say 'bout it all.'

'Sheriff Taylor?' Gramps mused. 'Ain't nothing he'll have to offer.'

'You see?' Nanna chimed. 'What did I tell y'all?'

The old man's nose was dancing as he drew closer. 'What's that cologne I smell? There some men folk here?'

There was a shuffle behind her. Lori watched as one of the boys slowly stepped forward.

'Sir,' he said, 'my name's Seymour. Charles Seymour. Now, if you'd just calm down and lower the gun, I'll explain to you how this here is just a big old misunderstanding, that's all.'

Gramps aimed the gun in the direction of

the voice. 'Stick your hands up, boy, or I'll blow your Got-damn mouth off!'

Charlie's hands shot up in the air. As did John C.'s. But Jake kept his hands by his side, a sudden smirk breaking across his lips. 'Ain't she gonna scold him for using foul language,' he muttered under his breath.

John C. chastised him with a hiss.

Gramps turned the gun towards Jake. 'Something funny, boy?'

Jake's hands shot up as if spring-powered. 'No, sir,' he said.

'No way this old coot is blind,' John C. muttered.

'Oh I assure you, son,' Gramps said, removing his glasses and opening his eyes wide for all to see. 'I ain't seen nothin' in many's a year.'

Lori knew those eyes all too well; milky white, with that tiny little black orb floating beneath each one.

'Get outta here!' John C. smiled. 'This is some kind of joke, right?'

Gramps slid the shades back over his eyes. 'Sure ain't no joke, son.'

John C. frowned, confused. 'I don't understand,' he muttered.

'And you'll do best to just leave it at that,' Gramps said.

He turned back to Charlie. 'You're the one was fooling around in the barn with my Lori. Ain't cha?'

Lori felt the color drain from her face.

Charlie was at a loss for words.

'That's right,' Gramps smiled. 'Thought you got one over on the poor old blind man, huh?'

Lori stepped forward.

'I'm sorry Gramps,' she said. 'We were just—'

'Quiet, girl!' he scolded. 'I sure am mighty disappointed in you. But we'll talk about that later.'

Gramps shifted his attention back to the guys. 'What you boys doin' round these parts?'

'Nothin',' Jake said.

'We came up here to hunt, sir, that's all,' John C. added.

'Oh, you're up here huntin' alright?' Gramps said, flashing a sly grin. 'Huntin' for a piece-a—'

'PAW!' Nanna yelled, silencing the old man. 'You ain't helpin' matters any.'

Jake sniggered.

Hackles raised, the old man backed off and lowered the shotgun. He slid a look to Jake, said, 'You can save your smiles for the law, son. God knows, the sheriff around these parts deserves nothing less.'

'I'll second that,' Roxy's voice chimed in. Everyone turned to watch as she entered the clearing. 'He ain't coming. Not today anyway.'

'Well, whadda ya know,' Nanna sneered. 'Good for nothing…'

'So we got ourselves a situation here, then,' Gramps said.

'Whaddayou mean?' John C. said. 'We told you it wasn't us.'

'That you did, son. And I suppose you're all entitled to due process.'

'Yeah. That's right,' Charlie said. 'Due process.'

'Still… Can't says I approve-a-you all snif-

102

fin' around my Lori and her friends like a pack-a-hungry dogs.'

Gramps aimed the gun slightly above head height, Lori covering her ears as he fired a single, deafening blast. The three men jumped, clawing their ears with their hands and turning tail to run.

'Now Git on outta here! Git!' the old man yelled. 'Cos my next shot's gonna be aimed at yo asses!'

The men seemed to quicken their pace at that, John C. even removing the Stetson and covering his ass with it as he retreated back into the woods.

Nanna was laughing. 'You got *fire* in your belly yet, old man!' she sang. 'Who'd have thought it?'

Lori looked to the mortified faces of Abby and Roxy and smiled weakly.

TWENTY

'Hold it,' John C. called to the others, 'They're heading back up the path.'

'What? All of them?' Charlie said, too scared to look himself.

'Yeah. Girls and all.'

The three men rested for a while under cover of the trees, still looking back from where they'd come.

'Jesus, that didn't go so well,' Jake said. He was still catching his breath, hands on knees. He was wheezing and made a mental note to cut down on the smokes.

Charlie glared at him, and then at John C. 'So which of you losers did the car over?'

Both men returned blank stares.

'Oh come on,' Charlie exclaimed, throwing his hands in the air. 'It must have been one of you clowns. Cos there ain't no one else around.'

'How do you know that?' John C. said.

'It *was* you,' Charlie pointed a finger accusingly.

'You must be joking."

'That Roxy chick shot you down, right? And you did the car over, like she said?'

'The hell I did. But I'm sure as hell going to do their campsite over. No bitch makes a fool out of John C. Lane and gets away with it.'

'I think we've done enough,' Charlie said. 'Let's just get out of here. We'll pack up tonight, hit the road early before the law rolls in. Dumbass sheriff or not, I've got my daddy's reputation to think of in all of this.'

Jake spat on the ground. 'Fuck your daddy,' he scowled.

'Excuse me?'

'I'm with John C. Ain't nobody gonna make a mule out of me and get away with it.'

'Alright, buddy,' John C. cheered. 'Let's do it.'

It didn't take them long to weave through the trees, discretely following the river towards the lake. The woods themselves were quieter than normal, as if the trees and the insects and the birds were all poised, waiting to see how the drama would unfold.

There was nobody around the girls' camp,

but their stuff still remained where they'd left it. The tent sat at the back of the clearing, the door-flaps unzipped exposing its innards. A rucksack lay half-opened, clothes and make-up and all manner of sparkly looking girly shit spewing out of its many pockets. Spent doobies circled the dead campfire.

'Fuckin' WHORES!' Jake cried, swinging his boot into the remnants of the campfire, scattering its blackened wood across the clearing.

He pulled the knife from his belt, ran it down the polyester skin of the tent, ripping a long, gaping hole.

'Now that's what I'm talkin' about,' enthused John C.

He found some empty bottles, lifted them and started to slam them against the ground, scattering glass across the site.

Charlie moved as the broken glass skittered around him. 'Guys, guys,' he complained, 'go easy!'

But the other two men were on a roll. Jake had found some firelighters in the rucksack. He ran his Zippo under one until it caught fire then threw it into the tent.

John C. cheered as the tent caught fire, grabbed the rucksack and threw it in for good measure. The remaining fire lighters followed.

'Burn, baby, burn!' Jake whooped, slapping skin with his buddy.

Charlie watched on bemused.

'Oh come on,' John C. goaded him. 'Lighten up, bro. Them ho's deserve it.'

'Maybe,' Charlie gave, 'but way I see it, you've just added more reasons for the law to come snooping around my daddy's place.'

'I told you what you can do with your daddy,' Jake mocked.

'My daddy's the reason why we're up here,' Charlie said. 'It's his truck, his gear. Every single shell we've been firing is registered under his name.'

'Well, ain't he a silly son of a bitch for letting you take it, then,' Jake laughed.

'He doesn't know, you idiot,' Charlie countered. 'And there ain't nobody would tell him until you guys went and trashed that car.'

'You watch your mouth,' John C. said. 'I'm just about sick of hearing about that mother fuckin' car, y'hear?'

'Jesus,' Charlie spat. 'Should have known not to get involved with a couple of rednecks.'

Jake laughed.

'Son,' he started, 'that's just about the best example of the pot calling the kettle black that I ever did hear. You may have a fancy college education and a pretty mouth with a silver spoon rammed down it, but deep down you're just as redneck as I am.'

The tent's outer sheet caught fire, an added roar escaping the blaze. John C. Lane danced around it like a man possessed, waving his Stetson in the air.

'And there ain't no question about his bloodline,' Jake quipped, laughing at his buddy.

Later, Charles Seymour packed his daddy's truck up, intent on leaving and putting as much distance between him and this Godforsaken place at the first sign of light. The other two men lay by the dwindling fire of their own camp up by the park, sleeping off the booze and badness. Empty bottles surrounded them. John C. slept with his Stetson covering his face.

Damn hicks, Charlie muttered, strapping the last of their gear into the back of the truck.

He made one last check around the camp but everything was pretty much scooped up and either burned, buried or stored in the back of the truck. Charlie had even retread their steps during hunting and scooped up what he could of the empty shells. He didn't want any sign left that he'd been here.

There was the matter of the couple they'd met a few days ago. The raven-haired house-wife and her fella with the camera. He had told them that his name was Charles, 'But most people call me Charlie,' he'd added. He had told the girls his name, too, so there wasn't much chance of coming out of this whole mess unscathed.

But Daddy wouldn't let him sink, even with all he'd done. They'd hire a good lawyer, may-be even pay those girls off. They looked the type to be persuaded by money, especially that slutty looking, mouthy blonde. And if that didn't work, Charlie could always sell the oth-er two out. Shame he wouldn't have another go with that Lori, fine as she was, and cool, too. It would've been nice to see where things might have gone after the weekend.

Charlie looked down at Jake and John C., still fast asleep.

Buddies my ass, he mused.

Had it not been for Happy Hour at Big D's

Lounge in Baton Rouge, bonding over drinks and stories that were most likely embellished, they would never have crossed paths in a million years and Charlie never would have considered a hunting weekend with these two hicks a good idea.

Charlie thought about grabbing a few winks himself before his trip, but he needed to take a piss first. He found a tree, stood in front of it, and unzipped his pants with intent. He let his head fall back, waiting for the inevitable relief. It came thick and fast, his bladder all but full. Charlie let out an obligatory 'Ah' sound as the stream continued to pour, steam rising up from the trunk he had chosen to stain.

He smelled something rotten, crinkled his nose at the offensive odor, thought,

Tha hell is that?

He looked down, eyes homing in on a mass withering of foliage spreading out from his feet. Dead weeds and grass, and the exposed roots of the mighty oak that towered over him. The old wood suddenly made a terrible crackling noise. Charlie watched open-mouthed as the roots twisted and writhed before him, a sickly hue traveling up to the base of the tree. There was a wailing sound from deep within its trunk as the desiccated brown hue continued to climb.

'What thaaa… fuck,' Charlie mouthed, high-stepping backwards out of the undergrowth.

As he watched, Charlie was able to decipher a pattern in the spread of creeping death up the tree. He traced it back to its source, which appeared to be coming from directly behind him.

But Charlie didn't have time to turn before a gloved hand clamped over his nose and mouth.

There was a flash of metal.

Charlie struggled to no avail as a knife blade bit into the soft flesh of his throat, and, sliding left to right, sliced through the subdermal layers and found purchase in his Adam's apple. The wound opened like a toothless, gummy maw, frothing and spitting blood.

Charlie dropped his cock and started choking. Both hands groped for the wound in his throat, blood seeping out between his fingers. He fell forward, at first to his knees and then head first into the sickly-colored tree trunk he was pissing over. He face-planted against its unyielding bulk, his bodyweight pushing forward and opening the wound even more. The impact spun him over, his head flopping like a limp-wristed wave. The ground smacked the remaining air from his body.

And there Charles Seymour rested, his life all but spilled across the newly dead foliage, and roots flexed in a five hundred year-old Louisiana Oak, blood and piss seeping out around his pretty boy mouth.

TWENTY ONE

'Supper's ready,' Nanna yelled up the stairs where Abby and Roxy were napping in one of the two bedrooms. Nanna had assigned the other room to Lori. She and Gramps would sleep on the couch.

Abby was the first one down the stairs. She looked out the window, yawning and stretching her arms, and reacted with surprise to how dark it had gotten.

'How long were we out?' she asked, running a hand through her hair to work out the tangles.

'Bout an hour and a half,' Gramps said as he fixed himself a plate.

Roxy appeared from behind Abby, rubbing her eyes. She muttered something by way of greeting, thought about having a smoke, then decided against it.

The small living area seemed even more cramped as Abby, Roxy, and the grandparents gathered for supper. Abby didn't mind, though. Right now, she needed to be around people and the more the better. That message scrawled on Lori's windshield was still bugging her. But the delectable aroma of Nanna's chicken and sausage gumbo pulled Abby out of her maudlin thoughts, making her stomach churn.

She stepped aside politely while Nanna fussed around with plates and cutlery. There were a million things to look at, propped up on shelves, mounted on the walls, and hanging from them. They ranged from interesting to downright creepy.

There wasn't enough room at the table, so Nanna served the girls at the table while she and Gramps had theirs on trays while sitting on the couch.

'Damn, that smells good,' Roxy said.

Normally, she preferred salads and fruit

cups, if anything at all, as she had her figure to watch: there was nothing worse than a fat stripper in Roxy's view. But right now she had the kind of appetite that could only be sated by something hearty, not rabbit food. And this shit looked hearty, if nothing else.

'What's in it?' she asked.

'Chicken, sausage, onion, green pepper, celery, chicken broth … and a few special ingredients, to make it mah own,' Nanna responded, like she had been waiting for someone to ask.

'It's really good,' Abby agreed. But she was just picking at her food, like a mouse. Working it around her plate.

Roxy was also playing it coy. She lifted a spoonful to her mouth, stuck her tongue out, snakelike and touched the tip of it to the spoon. She repeated the motion, stabbing further with her tongue this time, and then nodded approval. 'Not bad at all,' she said.

Nanna smiled proudly.

'Where's Lori?' Abby asked.

'She's still in a mood over that car of her's. Been out there the better part of an hour.'

'I told her not to wander too far,' Gramps chimed in.

'In a mood?' Roxy said. 'That's putting it lightly.'

'Something you should learn to do, young lady.'

Nanna pretended not to see Roxy roll her eyes.

'Well, I would be, too,' Roxy added.

Abby put down her spoon and started to get up from the table.' Maybe I should go see if she's—'

'You stay right where you are,' Nanna ordered. 'Best to Let Lori cool off.'

'You sure?'

'Trust me.'

Lori came in from outside five minutes later and ruffled at the ambush of concerned eyes on her. 'What?' she said.

'You alright?' Abby asked sheepishly.

'Not really,' Lori replied as she walked over to the stove and fixed herself a plate. 'Not much I can do about it right now, though, is there?'

Abby glanced over at Roxy, who shrugged and continued to eat.

For a time they ate and talked and everything was fine. Nanna regaled the group with a story about Lori's love of chicken and sausage gumbo. 'It's a wonder I'm not big as a house with all the good food she cooks,' Lori told them. It was like nothing had ever happened out there before.

After supper, Abby helped clean up while Roxy sneaked off outside for a smoke, Gramps following, muttering something about needing fresh air.

Nanna and Lori relaxed by the hearth.

'So what did you do to that poor girl?' Nanna scolded. 'What have I told you about foolin' with things you don't fully understand?'

'I'm not a kid anymore, Nanna,' Lori protested. 'I know what I'm doing.'

'Magic ain't somethin' you whip out to impress your friends.'

'It wasn't magic, Nanna. And I was trying to help Abby.'

'If you were foolin' around with nature, then it was magic. And your friend, there, she don't exactly look at peace, do she?'

'I'm fine, Nanna,' Abby said from the kitchen area, but just then the plate she was drying slipped from her hands and shattered across the floor.

Gramps stumbled through the door, Roxy right behind him. 'What's goin' on?' he called, shotgun at the ready. He looked to the kitchen, his brow furrowing, then said, 'You ain't right, girl. Them demons are tauntin' ye somethin' rotten.' He sniffed the air, waved the gun. 'I can smell 'em. YOU HEAR ME? I CAN SMELL YOU SONS OF—'

Abby froze, terrified of the old man.

Nanna rushed to calm him, stroking his hair and making soothing noises.

To Abby, she said, 'You ain't foolin' no one, child. Even old Gramps here can see that you're hurtin' somethin' awful.'

It was all too much for Roxy. 'Please,' she sighed, 'Can't we just talk about something normal for a change? This is all a little too *Twilight Zone* for me.'

Nanna's face twisted as she glared at Roxy. Her gums were working overtime, her lips slurping.

Roxy looked away, disgusted. *Old people*, she mused. *Gross.*

'I'm with Roxy,' Lori said. 'Let's just chill for a bit, all of us.' Her eyes fixed on Nanna, and narrowed. 'I've had enough lectures for one night.'

'You heed what your Nanna tells you,'

Gramps said. Nanna had settled him into his chair, but he still held the shotgun, un-cocked and drawn across his lap like a fat snake beset by rigor mortis. 'She's a powerful woman, your Nanna.'

'Oh go on with that ol' nonsense,' Nanna said, waving a hand as she returned to her own chair. 'Just want no harm coming to the girl. She's young and likes to try things she reads in those New Age books-uh-hers, but that stuff ain't child's play.'

'Oh for Chrissakes, Nanna. It's not like that at all!'

Nanna's voice rose: 'That's the problem with young' uns today,' she said, wagging her finger at Lori. 'Access to information ye shouldn't have. Get a book on just about anything nowadays and that ain't right. Some things have no business bein' written down, ain't that right, Paw?'

The old man made a noise that sounded like snoring. It probably meant he agreed.

Later, as the light waned and Nanna lit the downstairs lamps, Roxy leaned back in her chair and yawned.

'Think all that good food has made me sleepy,' she said.

'Well sleep, then, child,' Nanna snapped, blowing out a match

'I ain't sleepin',' the old man said.

'What ye mean you ain't sleepin'?' Nanna barked.

'I'm standing guard tonight,' he boasted. He puffed his chest out, snapped the barrels of his shotgun closed.

'Suit yourself, then,' Nanna shrugged. Yet a proud smile teased her lips.

'I'm just gonna grab some fresh air before bedtime,' Roxy said.

Gramps looked up hopefully but Nanna shot him daggers. Everyone in the room knew what fresh air meant.

Roxy tried to hide her smirk as she eased out of the cabin, alone.

The sun was now gone, the moon lauding proudly over the dark, shadowy forest. It was still warm. Roxy got away with wearing only a shirt and a denim miniskirt. She had untied the knot so that the shirt hung proper. The girls left all their clothes and things back at the camp but none of them were too keen on heading out to get them. *Hell*, Roxy thought. *I can sleep naked.*

But there'd be no sleep until her obligatory pre-bedtime cigarette. She'd have smoked something with a little more kick in it, were it not for the Grandparents, but the nicotine alone was doing its job.

Standing barefoot in the grass at the foot of the porch steps, Roxy let her head fall back and looked up at the starless sky. Under such a vast canvas of blues and purples, she felt small and insignificant. She was used to being boxed-in by skyscrapers, and she was quite fine with that. But tonight, just like the night before, a small part of her could appreciate this wide open space.

Roxy took one last drag of her cigarette and flicked the butt away. Suddenly, she was feeling uneasy again, the trees and the water and the air around her hostile and threatening.

And that fucking burlap man.

She would have to pass Geordi again on her way back inside. It would be about the forth or fifth pass since her arrival, and so far every time had been a chore. Her unease with the thing had no rhyme or reason. Sure, she knew it was harmless; nothing more than straw and burlap wrapped in old clothing. But Roxy couldn't shake the feeling that she was being watched in its presence.

As she started up the steps, Roxy's eyes regarded the burlap man thinly. She expected him to move, convinced that his posture was different from when she had last passed him. Once on the porch, she approached the thing with herky-jerky reluctance and stuck out her index-finger to poke Geordi's chest.

A dry wheezy sound escaped his straw filled coat. Roxy jumped back.

She waited, then leaned closer to his featureless face, listening more intently.   The cabin door opened, startling Roxy. She shot straight up and spun around.

'Ho-lee...' she said to Lori who walked out onto the porch unaware. 'You scared me!'

'I'm sorry,' Lori said, trying not to laugh. 'What were you doing?'

'Nothing.' Roxy said, embarrassed. But the excuse didn't fly. 'Nothing. *Really*!'

Lori looked over at Geordi and smiled knowingly. A semi-flustered Roxy headed for the door.

'Where you goin'?' Lori asked.

'Ahhh… *inside.*'

'Aw, c'mon,' Lori whined. 'Stay out here with me a little while longer.'

Roxy stopped at the door.

'Pleeease?' Lori cooed.

'Alright already,' Roxy said, then aimed a scowl at Geordi. 'But let's get off the porch, huh?'

'Tough day,' Roxy said as she and Lori walked down the porch steps and stood together in the grass.

Lori raised an eyebrow as if to say, *understatement of the year.*

She seemed colder than Roxy, goosebumps rising where the denim of her Daisy Dukes ended and the skin of her legs began. She wrapped both arms around her body, rubbed her hands up and down.

Roxy offered her a cigarette but Lori refused. 'Nanna doesn't know I smoke,' she added ruefully.

Roxy smiled at that. She reckoned Nanna knew damn well but didn't turn it.

The two girls stood, breathing in the night and all it had to offer. In many ways, they were very different people, and knew that. Yet in other ways, Roxy and Lori were quite alike. It was probably why they clashed so much. And probably why they had remained friends for so long despite the many arguments, debates, and offhand remarks to one another.

'So what is it between you and Nanna anyway?' Roxy asked Lori. 'She sure does have you wrapped around her little finger.'

Lori smiled. 'You know how I said Momma

and me lived down here 'til I was five?'

Roxy nodded.

'Well, the true fact of the matter was that Momma didn't do much of the rearing. It was Nanna and Gramps that raised me. At least in those early days. Momma wasn't quite up to it.'

Roxy could relate to that. She never even knew her own mom. Spent most of her early life being passed from pillar to post around extended family, most of whom she wasn't in touch with anymore.

'Anyway,' Lori continued, 'Nanna will talk it down but she's a very powerful woman. Round here she's what you might call a Mambo.'

'A what?'

'A Voodoo Queen, taught by a descendant of Marie Laveau, who was like the Madonna of Voodoo Queens back in the 1800s. The things I've seen Nanna do over the years,' Lori blew some air out, shook her head. 'Well, you just wouldn't believe it.'

'Probably not,' Roxy admitted emphatically as if to shout down the whiffs of self-doubt floating in the back of her mind. 'But I believe she cares for you, they both do. And so do I, Lori. I know I don't always show it.'

Lori locked arms with Roxy, leaned in on her shoulder. 'I know you do, girl. And I love you for it. You and Abby both.'

Roxy smiled, took another drag. With everything that had happened, she felt closer to those two girls than she'd felt to anyone else, period. From now on, they would deal with whatever came their way not just as friends, but as sisters.

'What happened back there?' Roxy asked. 'With you and Abby, I mean.'

Lori sighed. 'Nanna's right. I bit off more than I could chew. You know how Abby was talking about not feeling any release from what happened between her and Danny? Well, I tried to give her that release. Only maybe this was the wrong place to try it.'

'What do you mean, *wrong place*?'

'Oh just what Nanna was saying. There *is* something in those trees and in that lake, something that can be drawn upon. And I knew that. It's why I organised the trip here. I was planning to draw upon that energy to help Abby, only I think it may have been a mistake.'

Roxy looked away. 'Lori, you know I—'

'Don't believe in that stuff?' Lori finished for her. 'Right, I get that. But *I* do and *Abby* does. And what happened was real to *us*.'

'So tell me about it in words *I* can understand, then,' Roxy offered. 'I want to know what happened—'

'In *real* terms?' Lori continued. 'Alright, in *real* terms, Abby was still fucked up after last year. No amount of counselling or medication could ever fix that. But I couldn't watch her suffer anymore, Rox. I needed to try *something*. And Nanna's right, I should have been more careful, especially with Abby feeling wrong about this place from the very start, but I guess part of me thought that wasn't Abby talking, that it was Danny still inside her, still fighting.'

'So you're saying she was possessed by Danny?'

Lori looked behind her, making sure the

cabin doors and windows remained closed. 'I'm saying that when Abby stuck her knife into Danny's chest and killed that son of a bitch, that something of him entered her. That kind of thing can happen during traumatic events: I've heard of it before. And Abby wouldn't be truly free until it was exorcised from her. That bastard had haunted her enough when he was alive and I sure as hell wasn't going to let him do it in death. No way.'

They were quiet for a second, both girls looking out into the night.

'Did it work?' Roxy asked, finally.

Lori laughed. 'Oh it worked alright,' she said. 'We tore that bastard a new one, wiped every last trace of him out of her heart and soul.'

'But…' offered Roxy.

'But, in a place like this, messin' around like we did ain't exactly wise. It can unsettle things in the spirit world, stir up old grudges.'

Something caught Roxy's eye. Smoke rising up from within the trees and Roxy reckoned it was coming from the clearing where they were camping.

'Fuckin' *rednecks!*' she spat. 'They're torching our gear!'

Roxy started toward the wall of oaks.

Lori quickly followed. She grabbed Roxy by the shoulder, spun her around. 'What the hell do you think you're doing, girl?' she said.

'What does it look like? I'm going to put that damn fire out.'

'Right, with what? Your breath?'

'Don't be fuckin stupid.'

'Don't *you* be fuckin' stupid,' Lori scolded. 'You're always dissing me for being far-fetched or hippy or whatever. Well, marching out there on your own's gotta be the most stupid idea I've ever heard. There's something out there, Rox. And I don't know if it's human, *in*human or *super-fuckin'*-human, but it'll kick your ass either way.'

'So what do you say we do? Just sit here and watch those bastards torch all our stuff?!'

Lori looked beat. 'I don't know,' she offered. 'Ask Nanna?'

Roxy laughed humourlessly. 'What is *she* going to do?'

'Well I don't know! Let's ask and find out!'

'Ask who what?'

Both girls turned to find Nanna at the door.

Lori looked sheepish. 'Looks like someone's burning our stuff, Nanna.'

The old woman reached her glasses to her eyes, tried to find smoke across the treeline.

'Looks like *something*'s burning alright,' she said, 'But you can't tell *what* for sure.'

'It's them rednecks!' Roxy spat.

'That may be so, young lady, but it ain't something we can do anything about right now. So just settle yourself.'

'The hell with that,' Roxy fumed, heading towards the woods again.

'Or you could go get yourself raped and killed, maybe thrown on top of the tent or whatever else they got burning.'

Roxy stopped, turned.

'Your choice,' Nanna said. 'But Lori's staying right here.'

Lori sighed, looked once more to Roxy in appeal, then made back for the cabin. Once there she stood by the door with Nanna.

Roxy looked at both women again, and then at the burlap man, sitting there on his porch swing, seeming to mock her. Exhaling loudly, she followed Nanna and Lori inside making sure to look straight ahead.

'It ain't fair,' she complained.

'That it ain't,' Nanna agreed. 'That it ain't.'

TWENTY TWO

Roxy woke with a start.

Gramps' harmonica was warming up for the night, its haunting sound unwelcome in a place that already had its fair share of ghosts.

Roxy climbed out of bed and padded across the floor in the pitch dark, clashing with the spooky little knickknacks and Voodoo paraphernalia dangling from the walls and ceiling of the cabin.

The harmonica continued to wail. The barn was tonight's venue. The song was the same as last night's only muffled by the cabin walls.

Roxy groped her way to the bathroom, her eyes starting to adjust to the poor light. She pushed the door open, swept some more trinkets out of the way as she dipped inside the tiny room. There was a small sink against the rear wall facing the door, a medicine cabinet with a mirror door mounted above it. The toilet squeezed between it and an old-school bathtub with clawed feet. There was no shower. Apparently old black folks preferred taking baths.

It felt cooler in here, Roxy noticing the window above the toilet open. Standing knock-kneed, she attempted to pull it shut, but the damn thing was stuck, and she had to pee like nobody's business.

She looked at the toilet and a terrible image of Gramps perched on top of it flooded her mind. She swore quietly, unable to sit there, now, instead hawking down her panties and hovering over the damn thing. A mild euphoria set in as her bladder emptied.

A sound in the distance interrupted Gramps' wailing harmonica. It sounded like a car backfiring.

Or maybe a gunshot.

Roxy flushed the toilet and hiked her panties up. She lowered the toilet seat cover, knelt on top of it, and looked out the window. Her view was of the west side of the cabin; a wall of tall oaks silhouetted against a deep lavender sky. The wailing melody continued, bouncing off of the trees. The barn was located around back where Roxy couldn't see. Lori's car was on the other side of the treeline, in the small clearing before the woods grew thick and dense and darker than she cared thinking about.

Roxy waited for another interlude in the harmonica's song and then focused her hearing toward the woods facing the front of the cabin, where she assumed the sound had come from.

Nothing.

She waited for a while until Gramps' harmonica kicked into another song. Then she climbed down from the toilet, washed her hands and made her way back to her room in the paling dark.

She came to Lori's room. The door was slightly ajar. Roxy pushed the door open and leaned inside. It was darker in there, no windows.

'Hey! Lori! You awake?' she whispered, but apparently her friend was fast asleep. 'Lori! You awake?' she called louder this time.

'I'm right here,' came a voice from behind. Roxy whipped around and saw Lori standing at the top of the stairs. She was dressed as if she'd been out. 'Keep your voice down or you'll wake up Nanna!'

'Fuck, man!' Roxy complained. 'I'm starting to think you enjoy doing that.'

Lori chuckled, shot back a sarcastic, 'Yeah.'

'I thought you were sleeping,' Roxy said.

'I *couldn't* sleep. Was hanging out with Gramps in the barn.'

'Did you hear something a few minutes ago?'

'Like what?'

Roxy paused, about to describe what she thought she'd heard.

'Never mind,' she said finally, and then walked toward her room. 'Goodnight.'

Sleep took her quickly. She dreamed vividly, all the crazy things she'd seen in this place: the woods and the cabin and ol' Geordi the burlap man.

She awoke again, this time to shouting.

Roxy heard the old man's voice from living room. From outside, she heard another male voice, high-pitched, panicked, and familiar.

As her eyes adjusted to the dark, Roxy noticed Abby in the corner, cowering, Lori trying to soothe her.

'What the…?' she began but Lori shushed her.

'Shit's hitting the fan out there,' she said. 'Sounds like that guy, John C.'

'Tha hell's wrong with him?' Roxy said, pulling herself out of bed and into her skirt. She found her shirt, threw it on.

'Just let Gramps handle it,' Lori said. 'He's got the gun.'

'Tha hell with that,' Roxy countered, slipping into her cowboy boots and stomping toward the door.

'Roxy, leave it!' Lori yelled at Roxy's back, but she kept on walking right out of the room.

Roxy ran into Nanna on the stairs. The old woman carried a lamp, on her way up to warn the girls. She wore a flowered night dress, Bugs Bunny slippers, and her hair was wrapped in a scarf. It almost looked like some kind of crown.

'Go on back to your room now, child,' she said to Roxy. 'It's not safe down there.'

'Not safe?' Roxy said, craning to see over the old woman's shoulders.

'I told you to get away from that window,' Nanna yelled at the old man. Then back to Roxy, 'Old fool's gonna get himself killed.'

Still grumbling, Nanna lifted her night dress with her free hand and trundled down the stairs.

Roxy followed.

Downstairs, Gramps stood by the window,

the shotgun in his hand. He turned as Roxy and Nanna came down, shooed them both away.

'Get back in your rooms,' he called. 'I'll handle this.' His voice was loose and gummy, and Roxy realized he didn't have his teeth in. He wasn't wearing his shades either, pearl white eyes baggy in his head like he'd just woken.

Nanna hurried over to the old man and tried to pull him away.

'Come on, now,' she said. ''Fore you get yourself killed.'

Gramps went to protest, but the old woman outweighed him by about thirty pounds. They stumbled away from the window, a clumsy mass of flailing limbs and bad balance.

Roxy sidled up to the window, peered out.

John C. Lane was outside the cabin, at the foot of the porch. He looked like hell, his trademark Stetson nowhere to be seen, his plaid shirt ripped and bloodied. He was crying like a baby, pleading for them to let him in.

'Don't let him in,' Roxy said.

'Oh don't you worry, child. He ain't coming nowhere near us,' Nanna assured.

'I'll shoot yo ass!' Gramps yelled at John C. 'So you git on outta here!'

'Please,' the redneck begged. 'You have to let me in. She's still out there.'

'Who's still out there?' Roxy yelled.

'Christie Keller!' he returned. 'She's killed the others and she's coming for me!'

TWENTY THREE

The mere mention of Christie Keller seemed to spark something within the old man. He pulled free from his wife's grip, striding back over to the window like a man sixty years his junior, those milky, white eyes bulging from his head.

He lifted the shotgun, straining his ears before aiming both barrels squarely at John C.

'You wanna tell me that again, son?' he said.

John C. was beside himself.

'Look, I ain't lying to you, old man! It was Christie Keller.'

'Christie Keller, you say,' Gramps mused. 'What makes you say a damn thing like that?'

'I say it cos it's the truth! Please,' John C. begged. 'Either help me or shoot me cos I ain't going back near those woods. Fact, I ain't going nowhere.'

'Ain't that the truth,' Roxy quipped.

She checked the door to the cabin, made sure it was locked tight.

But in that moment, Gramps lowered his gun. He turned to the old woman, shook his head, then fished the rope-necklace from under his shirt and rubbed its pendant between his thumb and index finger.

'Let the boy in,' he said to Roxy.

Roxy couldn't believe her ears. 'What?! You *crazy*, old man?'

'Let him in, I said.'

Roxy looked to Nanna, who simply stepped aside. 'If the man says let him in then let him in.'

'Oh for Christ's sake!' Roxy protested.

'Stand aside,' Gramps said, gently moving Roxy out of his way.

He felt around the wood with his palms, unlatched three locks and two bolts, then opened the door.

John C. was in within seconds, shivering in the doorway, looking traumatised. But Roxy wasn't convinced. She raised two painted fingers to her eyes then pointed them at the redneck.

'I'm watching you,' she said.

'Come on,' Nanna said, pulling the boy on through the cabin, 'let's get you warmed up. And then you're gonna talk, boy. And it best be good.'

Abby was the last one down after John C. had come into the cabin. All eyes were on her as she descended the creaky wooden stairs. Her face was flushed, her eyes hiding behind the lenses of her wireframes.

'What?' she asked, sliding into a chair by the fire.

'We're all just worried about you,' Lori said.

'Well don't be,' Abby said. 'I'm fine.' She smiled as if to show how fine she was, but it wasn't convincing anyone. 'Seriously!' she exclaimed, not happy with all the unwanted attention.

John C. set his mug down. He dug further into the blanket Nanna had given him and ran his eyes over the cabin's peculiar decor. To Roxy, he looked like some overgrown mole sitting there.

'That okay for ye?' Nanna asked him, taking the mug and carrying it over to the kitchen area.

'It's great. Thanks.'

'Want any more?'

'No, I'm good.'

Nanna returned to her chair, settled into it.

'Well, let me be the judge of that,' she said.

A silence descended upon the room, all eyes off Abby and onto the young man in the chair.

'Remind me of your name, cowboy,' Nanna said.

'John C. Lane, ma'am,' he said, polite as a butler.

'Well, Mr Lane,' I want you to start from the beginning, then, and tell us exactly what happened out there and whose blood that is on your shirt.'

John C. didn't want to remember what happened out there. He wanted to forget. But he knew that wasn't likely. Not for a long, long time. Maybe not ever. He'd once heard that talking about a traumatic event, thus purging oneself of it, was the best way to cope with such a thing. So John C. did exactly that...

'I ain't no angel,' he began. 'Did a few things I ain't proud of in my life. My daddy left when I was young, but Momma brought me up as a good Christian and I should act like one more of the time. But I don't and I ain't gonna pretend otherwise. You want the truth and I'll give it to you as I see it. I'll lay it out nice and neat.'

He shifted in his chair, pulled the blanket even closer. It was hard to be cold in this part of the world and the cramped living area of the cabin, but still John C. shivered.

Roxy wasn't fooled by the bad boy come good routine.

'Did you trash Lori's car?' she asked.

'No,' he said.

Roxy rolled her eyes.

'But I *did* trash your campsite,' John C. nervously revealed. 'We, I should say...'

'What did you just say?' Lori spat.

'I said, we trashed your campsite. Burned your tent and everything. But only after trash talkin' from *her*.' One hand appeared from John C. Lane's blanket and pointed straight at Roxy.

'Oh, it's my fault that you burned our stuff? Well, ain't that something.'

'Let the boy talk,' Nanna ordered. 'What's done is done. We can sort it out with the law tomorrow. But burning tents don't get blood on a man's clothes, does it now?'

The cowboy dipped his head. 'No, ma'am,' he said. 'That was Christie Keller did that.'

'Did you actually see the girl?'

He looked up again and nodded. 'On the lake...' he said as if the memory played out before his eyes. 'She was... dancing on the lake.'

'Give me a brea—' Roxy started to say until Nanna thrust her hand toward the girl, silencing her.

'I had gone down to the lake to refill the wash bucket when I saw her,' John C. continued. 'Those eyes. They were there. In the water. Looking right at me. And then she was gone.'

John C. was met with a roomful of quizzical expressions, save for Roxy, who was pissed at the level of naïveté on display, and Abby, who appeared to know something about what the terrified man was going on about.

'I thought I was seeing things,' he continued, 'but then she appeared again. I started to run. I looked back and saw her dancing on the surface out in the middle of the lake like... like Jesus walkin' on water or something. Ol' Christie was flickering in and out like a firefly. Each time she'd appear somewhere different. And then she appeared in the woods. Musta been ten or twenty feet away. I ran as fast as I could.'

The room was silent.

Roxy glared at John C. She could feel her face burning red. She had issues with Nanna for cock-blocking her and she had issues with everyone else in the room for buying this asshole's story.

'They say Christie possessed them folks back in the day,' John C. said. 'Made them do her biddin'. Well, that's how it was tonight. She had someone with her. Musta been guiding him somehow.'

Nanna traded eyes with the others before returning to John C. Lane. 'What did this someone look like?'

'He wore an overcoat and had this big, fancy cane knife,' John C. said, using his hands as a visual aid. 'He had on some kinda mask made out of burlap that covered his whole head, but it didn't have no eye-holes or a mouth or nothing. And it had this weird writing all over it that was moving the whole time.'

'Wait a minute. What!?' Roxy interrupted, a confused scowl on her face.

The others had caught on too.

Lori hurried over to the front door, opened it, and looked out onto the porch. 'He's not there,' she said a second later.

Roxy followed Lori over to the door. 'Whatdayou mean, he's not there?'

'I mean Geordi's not there.'

Roxy pushed her friend aside and looked for herself.

'Alright!' Roxy said, sticking her head back in. 'What, the hell is going on here—'

'Language, child,' Nanna scolded.

'I think maybe somebody's trying to put one over on us,' Gramps suggested. He turned to John C. and said, 'You wouldn't know anything about that, wouldju?'

'No sir.'

'It makes perfect sense,' Roxy said, running with the thought. 'First they vandalize the car. Then they trash our campsite and burn our tent. Then they swipe the dummy and try to scare us with this Christie Keller BS. His friends are probably out there laughing at us right now.'

'Stop it, Roxy,' Lori mumbled, deadfaced, as if she had not intended to speak it aloud.

'What dummy?' John C. asked, but his voice was lost in Roxy's accusatory rambling.

'It *had* to be them,' she was saying . 'It…er Geordi certainly didn't get up and walk away on his own.'

'I said STOP IT!'

The room became quiet.

Lori was standing by the door pushing air through flared nostrils. She appeared more frightened than angry. Roxy took solace in that. Looking around the room, it was clear to her that the others shared Lori's sentiment. Roxy pretended to zip her mouth shut.

'What dummy?' John C. asked again.

The old man's eyes were wide with concern.

He leaned in close to the cowboy and mused, 'You said she was guiding it. What, exactly did she *guide it* to do?"

John C. dry swallowed. He closed his eyes.

'The guy in the burlap mask... he was fighting with Jake when I walked up on em'. You've seen Jake. He ain't no small guy, and he definitely ain't one to back down from a fight, but this guy, this burlap man was tossin' him around like a ragdoll. Each time he would stand there and wait for Jake to pick himself up off the ground before kicking the shit out of him again and again, like he was just toying with him.'

'Why didn't you help him?' Roxy said.

John C. hesitated, guilt bubbled to the surface and left him tongue-tied.

'Go on,' Gramps said.

'That burlap man got Jake down one last time and started hackin' away at him with the cane knife. Just cuttin' him to pieces right there in front of me, like meat on a butcher's block. The way Jake was screaming... I never knew a grown man could sound like that.' John C. stopped to swallow the hot lump in his throat. 'I know I shoulda done something, but I was so scared,' he said, his voice trembling. 'So I ran. That's when I found Charlie sprawled on the hood of the truck with his throat cut from ear to ear. He had this look on his face, like… like he might still be alive. I pulled him off, tried to wake him up.' John C. glanced at the stain on his shirt. 'That's where the blood came from.'

You could hear a pin drop in the room. Even Roxy was quiet.

'I just couldn't believe what I was seeing,' John C. continued. 'I kept thinking, it has to be a dream. It *has* to be a dream. But it wasn't. When I looked up, the burlap man was standing over Jake's body. Just standing there facing me, you know. There was this like… heat coming off him, like when you see it rising from a car engine on a hot day. Things were dyin' all around him, like he was toxic or something. And the smell. I don't know how to describe it except to say it smelled like death.'

Roxy laughed, but it was a nervous laugh. 'Rrrright…'

'It's true,' John replied. 'I don't know how to explain it. The grass. The shrubs. The tree-bark. Even Jake's clothes and skin was affected. It was the strangest thing…' He trailed off and stared blankly into space.

'So then what happened?' Lori said, snapping John out of his trance.

'I made a move like I was gonna run, and he moved too. I froze and he froze. Like it was all just a game to him. It went on like that until I finally just hightailed it into the woods and hid.'

'Come onnn,' Roxy said. 'What is it with you people and this Christie Keller chick? It's just some story, right?'

'You're not from around here,' John C. scolded. 'If you were, you'd know all about

Christie Keller and you'd have some respect for what I'm telling you.'

Roxy fixed him a look. 'So educate me,' she said.

'Christie Keller ain't no laughing matter,' Gramps piped up. 'She's a part of the history in these parts, that much is true. But not many people like to talk too much about what gone on, me included.'

'Would someone *please* tell me what the big fuc... freakin' deal is with this chick?''

Nanna shot Roxy a sour look. 'I'll tell you,' she said.

The old woman took a sip from her mug, got herself comfortable, then began.

'Christie Keller was the daughter of a couple of church-goin' negro folks, as black as Gramps and me,' she said. 'Only Christie was born white. Whiter than white, with skin that was almost luminous, and hair like the snow you see in those Christmas cards they sell down at the market every year. Even her eyes were pale, a shade of gray so light that you'd have thought they were glowin' when she looked at you.'

'So, she was Albino,' Roxy said. 'I've seen some pictures of black Albinos. They still have black features, only their skin's white.'

'No. Christie weren't no black Albino. The doctors at the time said it was a freak of genetics or somethin' but most reasonable folks round here understand what was really going on.'

'And what was that?'

'She was mixed,' Lori spoke up and, for a split-second, stole the spotlight.

'Yes. Well, that's a story for another time,' Nanna said. 'Either way, the Kellers took little Christie home and loved her just like they should have. It was other folks that created problems for the poor girl.

'It all started in school, as you could expect. Kids teasing her, pushing her around. One day Christie finally decided she had enough and dished out a little payback at her tormentors. The parents got all up-n-arms, complaining about how the devil child struck out at their little angels. And with the teachers being as freaked out by Christie as everyone else, there weren't nobody going to stand up for her.

'So she left school early. Her Paw was a farmer, just like his Paw before him, but Momma ran a laundering business and I guess Christie helped out with that. Either way, she rarely came into town, stayed at their old place on the outskirts and kept herself pretty clean.

'Cept one night, a white boy called Joseph got himself in a tangle with some out of town girl. She was from a couple of towns east of here and her folks turned up saying all kinds of things about that boy. How he beat their little girl and raped her and left her for dead.'

Roxy looked to Abby. This wasn't going to do her mental health any good. Talk about getting away to the country, being at one with nature and all?

Nanna continued: 'Well, the law was gonna throw everything at the boy. He'd done a number on that girl for sure, even found teeth marks all over her arms and legs and private parts. But his own mommy and daddy didn't think their little boy could do something like that, so they looked to some other influence. They were Bible thumpin' folks, you see...'

'Evangelicals,' Gramps corrected.

'They were tight with the local preacher, too,' Nanna continued, unabated. 'Reverend Waters was his name. So next thing you hear, the boy's saying he was possessed by some demon, that it weren't his fault. But the girl's folks were having none of that, until the boy started naming names, saying that Christie Keller had seduced him one night and he'd lay with her and she'd put a demon inside him.

'Well after that, pretty much everyone and their dog starts comin' outta the woodwork saying Christie Keller's put a demon in them. Poor girl was blamed for everything from bad debt to spoiled milk. It was like Salem all over again. Finally, a group of women got themselves together and went to the Kellers' house. They took that young girl, dragged her down to the lake, and killed her.'

Roxy shook her head. 'That's just insane.'

'It's what happened, young lady. Those women drowned Christie Keller right by that lake you young'uns are camping by. Lori's Gramps has been fussin' about it since you all came here. Keeps standing by the window, asking me to look outside and tell him everything's okay. Course, he don't know we can't see the lake no more from the cabin, not since the trees have all grown up. But I tell him everything's okay anyway, just to put his mind at rest.' She smiled affectionately at the old man, but he didn't return it. Looked like Gramps was just about sick of being patronised.

'Okay, poor little Christie drowned. So what?' Roxy said. 'You've said yourself how a lot of stuff has gone down round the lake over the years. What makes this so special?'

'Nobody talked much about the details less'n they incriminate themselves. But supposedly Christie Keller cursed all the women involved with her dying breath, but nobody was willin' to say one way or the other. There was a real sense of dread surrounding the whole thing. Still is to this day. We take things like curses seriously around here.'

'Ya think?' Roxy remarked under her breath.

'It's what happened afterwards that gives the story teeth, you see. Despite what took place down at the river, poor Christie was given a proper Christian burial. Probably to keep the parents quiet, and to put God between the curse and guilty parties. Word of the curse sent the town into a panic. The women involved were shunned. Most folks assumed it was only a matter of time before ol' Christie came-a calling. And by God were they right.'

'What do you mean?' Abby pressed, hanging on Nanna's every word.

'The first time it happened, they thought nothing of it. Old Pete Crowe was a drinker anyway, so I guess they put it down to that. But he beat his wife until she didn't breathe one night, killed her stone dead. And Betty Crowe was no mouse of a woman. Known to keep old Pete in line, shall we say, up until that night.

'And then it happened again, young Lucy Holder getting done in by her old man. Now

Cecil Holder was like one of those reeds you see growing on the bayou; a strong breeze coulda knocked him over. Quiet fella, kinda bookish looking, yet he went to town on his old lady one night, bitin' and scratchin' like some wild animal.

'Word started spreadin' that Christie Keller's curse was at fault. That each night the moon turned red, ol' Christie opened the doors of hell and let some demon out to possess those men, getting revenge on the women who killed her.'

Everyone turned to look at John C. Lane again.

'I ain't possessed by nobody,' he said. 'You can forget *that* right now.'

'So what, then?' Roxy spoke to everyone, but especially to John C., and Nanna. She was pointing toward the front porch. 'Christie Keller possessed the stupid dummy—'

'Fetish,' Gramps corrected, cutting her off.

'*Sorry*. That stupid *fetish*... Geordi or whatever his name is?'

Nanna laughed. 'The whole thing's a loada bunk.'

Roxy exchanged a confused look with Abby.

Nanna continued: 'Them heffers killed an innocent young girl that night, simple as that. I reckon outright murder didn't sit right with them, so they turned poor Christie into a villain to make themselves feel better about what happened out there on the river bank. Truth be told, she weren't even a witch. But I guess that played better with townsfolk at the time. You know how white folks do, 'specially back in the day. There ain't no blood red moon and there ain't no demon possessin' our burlap man. The way I see it, Paw is right about this young man here spoonin' us a load of BS.'

Roxy's eyes lit up. 'Well, it's about time—'

Nanna shushed her with short hissing sound.

'Wha?' said a dismayed John C. He motioned toward the old woman.

Gramps aimed his shotgun at the cowboy, and he threw his hands up in surrender.

'I'll give you points for that bit about La Vapeur du Démon,' Nanna said to the cowboy. 'Not many people know about that.'

'The what?' Roxy whined in a high-pitch.

'The Devil Vapor,' Nanna said. 'It's the aura that surrounds dark magic. It laughs at the laws of nature, giving life to inanimate objects or taking it from living things. It is said that nothing can escape its indelible touch.'

'*Ohhhhh*. The Devil Vapor,' Roxy mocked.

Nanna's eyes narrowed in contempt.

'Yeah, and wouldn't we see some sign of the vapor outside the cabin?' asked Lori.

'This place is protected,' Nanna said. 'The barrier outside would weaken any dark magic that comes near it. That might explain why you wouldn't see signs of the vapor.'

'But someone couldn't cross the barrier, right?' Lori said. 'In theory...'

'That would depend on how powerful that someone is.'

'But what if they did?'

'Their power would be compromised at the very least.' Nanna gave Lori a look that was enough to close the conversation right down.

'I told y'all the truth,' John C. interjected. 'There's no way I could make up a story like that!'

But Gramps just sat there, holding the gun on him, a gloating smile hovering below his dead, white eyes.

'Whatever the case, we'll get the law up here in the morning and get to the bottom of this,' Nanna said. 'By hook or by crook.'

TWENTY FOUR

Sheriff Sam Taylor stood by the porch of his summer house, beer in one hand and smoke in the other, watching the early morning sun work its way across the sky.

The letter was pinned to the porch railings, levelled down with an old rock from Sam's overgrown garden. He must have read it a hundred times by now, but there were still some parts he couldn't digest too well no matter how much beer he tried to wash it down with.

The alimony.

That was a word he knew all too well from dealing with domestics over the years, enforcing court judgements with men all too willing to shirk responsibility or disappear into the undergrowth. Of course, he might have more sympathy for those poor bastards now after reading Whitney's letter because what she was trying to hit him for seemed good enough reason for turning a hand. Crime may not pay at the end of the day, but it sure could top up his measly sheriff's wage. And Sam was going to need every penny he had were he to keep himself watered and fed if what this letter was proposing was anyway right.

Five hundred dollars? A month?!

Sam wasn't a saver, never had been. Whitney had looked after all that sort of thing, tucking a little away each month in her own little savings account. They'd dip into it for rainy day expenditures such as leaky roofs and the like. Course, now that little pot of gold was gone, the roof stayed leaky. Until, that was, one of his ever loyal supporters came round to fix it. Usually someone from the bar. Drinkers were good that way: regular little Santa's helpers the lot of them.

Sam dragged on his cigarette. Read the letter again. Then thought about what Tom had told him in the bar, about the eighteen year-old kid he'd had working the lawn.

Eighteen, for Christ Sakes!

Screwing a cop's wife. It would take some balls to do that.

The boy's name was Julian and he'd no bigger balls than your average kid. He'd just graduated high school and had his sights set on college on the East Coast – Pittsburgh or Philly. Sam couldn't remember which. What he did remember was selling Whitney on the boy, thinking that she would complain about more money being spent on services they didn't need.

'Seems like a good kid,' Sam had said. 'Good head on his shoulders. Says he's going to use the money for college books and such. You're always talking about giving back to the community.'

To which Whitney replied, 'He's got parents. Let them buy his books.'

Sam shuddered at the memory of his next response. 'Well at least you'll have some eye candy during the day.'

'Gee thanks,' she replied sarcastically.

Like Whitney would ever, in a million years, carry on with an eighteen year-old, or even a twenty five year-old for that matter! Whitney liked her men to be men, with a good helping of gravitas, like Sam used to possess before marriage, the job, and ultimately alcohol had taken its toll. At least he thought she did.

None of it made any sense to Sam in the real world.

Where did it all go wrong?

Hell, it was the cliché to end all clichés. But it was exactly what was going through his head . *Where did they go wrong?*

He remembered things being good. The ring, the wedding, their first year as man and wife. Yeah, things were very good. But now, as he sifted through those memories, he wondered if they'd been somewhat glamorized over the years, given a little fairy dust by all the booze that soaked his brain. Was it always bad between them? Were they once just better at hiding it?

Who knows? Who cares?

Sam did.

He heard his phone ringing in the kitchen. He wondered vaguely who it could be this early, then dismissed the thought outright: Edna had taken to ringing him at home lately, instead of on the car's two-way, what with his office (and car) hours being less than regular. He had no intention of answering it but the ringing gave him an idea about what the hell to be doing with his day.

Sam looked at the letter once more, downed the rest of his beer then flicked the cigarette stub out into the yard. He retreated back into the house looking for his phone book.

This hearing he had to attend... He was going to need a lawyer.

'Did you get him?' Roxy asked Nanna.

'Nope. But the woman I did get said she'd send someone up right away, even if she has to go to the city to do so.'

'That'll take hours.'

'Well, it's all we got,' Nanna said.

Abby was sitting in the living area, wrapped up in one of Nanna's shawls. It was an ugly thing that reeked of old people, but it kept her warm. She had taken off her glasses and the bags under her eyes looked heavy in the early morning light creeping through the window.

'It's not right,' she said, looking over at both Nanna and Roxy. 'It feels like there's no one to help, like we're completely on our own out here.'

'That's country living,' Nanna said. 'And it's usually a good thing not to be bothered by the law.'

'Well, it doesn't feel good right now,' Abby said.

'We could walk into town,' Roxy said. 'Grab

the next bus back to the city.'

'No way,' a voice said, Lori coming down the stairs. 'I ain't leaving Nanna and Gramps.'

'Oh hush, child, we'll be okay!' Nanna insisted. 'Lived through a lot of bad times round these parts and this ain't no different!' But the look in her eyes betrayed her.

The door opened, all heads turning at its sound. John C. Lane came in first, a towel wrapped around his shoulders, his hair wet and his face red. Gramps came behind him, shotgun wedged into John C's back.

'So when they picking the boy up?' the old man asked.

'Taylor ain't in yet,' Nanna said. 'They'll send to the city if he don't make it through the door in the next hour.'

'Typical,' Gramps said.

John C. found a seat in the living area, sat himself down. He unwrapped the towel, folded it and sat it on the coffee table next to him. He looked at Nanna, said, 'I got nothin to fear from Sheriff Taylor. I ain't done nothin' wrong.'

'Bullshit,' Roxy said.

'You believe what you like, but that's the God's honest truth. I'm guilty of huntin' where the law says I ain't allowed and I'm guilty of damagin' your property, on account of bein' misrepresented, but I ain't no killer.'

'Show us,' Roxy said.

'What?'

'There's a guy comes into the club every Thursday. Likes a private dance from yours truly. Anyway, we got to talking and he tells me he used to be a cop. Worked homicide for years, says anyone could tell a killer from the way they look at the scene of the crime.' Roxy looked squarely at John C. Lane. 'So I say we march on down to that camp and see what your sorry ass looks like.'

'I ain't goin down there for no—'

'Wait a minute,' Lori cut in. 'You mentioned a truck earlier."

John C. shook his head. 'So...'

'Well, it's probably big enough to take us into town, right? So we can all go see the sheriff in person, straighten this thing out once and for all.'

TWENTY FIVE

The woods were quiet. The air was still, not even a breeze blowing. The birds called out to each other in low mournful murmurs. Even the waters seemed muted, their flow less urgent.

John C. Lane led the way. Roxy and Gramps followed, both linking arms, the old man's shotgun aimed squarely at the redneck's back.

They went to the girl's camp first. It was a mess. The tent had burned to the ground, just like John C. had said, most of the girls' stuff gone with it.

'Bastard,' Roxy seethed.

'I ain't proud of what I done,' John C. conceded, 'but you pissed me off, girl.'

The boys' camp was largely untouched. The remnants of a fire stood pride of place in the centre, a metal spit arched over it. The tent was

146

still there, next to the spit, its open flap revealing a couple of sleeping bags, some magazines and hunting gear inside.

But then, on the ground nearby…

Swatches of dead foliage and shrubs charted an indiscriminate path that appeared to have been travelled in haste. From the base of a nearby tree, roots infected with mold and decay twisted into painful shapes. The tree bark was rotted. Several pointed branches protruded from the earth like spindly insect legs.

'Look. There.' John C. pointed at the diorama of dead and dying woodland.

Roxy, who had already spotted the improvised pathway, shrugged and said, 'Doesn't mean anything. You guys could've done that.'

'How, the hell, would we have—'

'I don't know. Maybe you took a torch to it or something,' Roxy said as she helped Gramps sit himself down on an old log, and then followed the pathway of dead earth over to the boys' truck parked nearby.

She gingerly approached the driver side of the vehicle. John C. went to join her.

'You stay right here with me,' Gramps warned.

From his perch, the old man began sniffing the air. He locked onto a curious scent and straightened up, brow creasing. He secured his grip on the shotgun. Something weren't right here.

As she moved closer to the truck, Roxy could see a stripe of crimson smeared down the hood. Her eyes widened.

'They were over there,' John C. pointed to a

rucksack lying off centre in a dead swatch near the back of the campsite. He'd found his Stetson and clutched it in his hands like a security blanket, his body shaking, fresh tears breaking from his eyes. 'The burlap man threw Jake on the ground and started goin' to town on him with the cane knife. The s-sound of that blade going into his flesh...'

John C. looked to Roxy, and then to the truck.

'Charlie was laid out on the hood,' he said, sniffling. 'That smear you see is his blood. I tried to pull him free but he was gone already.'

But Roxy wasn't buying it. The hum of fresh bullshit once again filled her nose. *The blood on the car is animal blood – probably from a raccoon.*

'Hundred bucks says that blood ain't even human.'

John C. made a face. 'What the hell are you talking about?' he said.

'Where is he, then? Where's the body?' Roxy folded her arms, glared at the redneck. 'The other guy, too. Jake or whatever his name was.'

'How the hell would I know? I told you, I ran.' John C. turned to Gramps in appeal. 'I swear, it happened just like I said. Christie must've moved the bodies.'

Roxy was shaking her head. Her eyes surveyed the nearby trees finding blood splashed across them like red paint.

'This is *so* fucked up,' she thought aloud. 'So majorly fucked up. I don't know about you, Gramps, but I don't trust this guy. We should ditch his lyin' ass right here and now.'

John C. threw his hands into the air. 'Jesus

H. Christ! What do I have to do to make you people understand that I didn't do this?'

The old man was going over options in his head. He settled on one, and then said, 'Fraid she's right, son.'

'Wha? You can't be serious.'

'I don't want you anywhere near them girls. Now, I ain't gonna ditch you but I ain't havin' you in the cabin neither. You'll stay in the barn until Sheriff Taylor drags his lazy bones up here.'

'No! Please! I don't wanna be left alone,' John C. begged. 'You can't leave me alone.'

'Calm down, boy. It's just for a couple hours.'

'A couple hours? It took just a couple seconds for that... *thing* to kill Jake. Christie Keller's coming for me, too, you know.'

Roxy shook her head, rolling her eyes for the millionth time.

'You listen here, boy,' Gramps tightened. In an instant his cool demeanor shifted, a tinge of fear floating beneath his angry face. 'Maybe my wife don't believe in the legend, but I do. And I don't appreciate you and your friends makin' light of it.'

'No. I swear—'

'I heard you the first time, son,' Gramps said. He shoved the barrel forward, poking John C. in the chest like it was his index finger. 'Now, if it comes out that this is all some big joke, I'll shoot every last one-ah you fools ma-*d-a-m-n-* self. Ya hear?'

'Might as well just admit it, dude,' Roxy instigated.

'I am so *sick* of hearing your voice,' John C.

growled.

'Well, that's too damn bad because—'

They heard the sound of Grandpa's shotgun being cocked. Roxy turned around just in time to see the old timer standing and pointing his gun into the forest. He fired off a shot. The blast was deafening, its shell rattling against the thick, dense blanket of wood and fern. A couple of birds cried out in protest then fluttered away.

Gramps aimed again.

'Jesus,' Roxy cried. 'What the hell are you doing?'

But the old man was spooked, listening intently for something then firing off a second round. He started feeling around his pockets for more shells.

'Stop it,' Roxy cried. 'There's nothing out there!'

'Oh, there's s-something out there alright,' Gramps stuttered. I can feel it. Damn, girl, I can *hear* it. Moving in those trees, laughing at us, making fools of us.'

He dropped his shells, swore, then fell to the ground, feeling desperately for them.

Roxy grabbed the gun.

John C. tried to help the old man to his feet, but Gramps pushed against him. 'Leave me be!' he protested. 'There's something out there, I know it.'

'He ain't wrong,' the cowboy said. 'We got to get out of here.'

Roxy thought for a moment, weighing things up. The gun was uselessly poised in her hands. She ran her eyes across the woods in front of them, homing in on the dead foliage and black-ened tree bark.

'You got the keys to that thing?' she asked John C., looking back to the truck.

'No, but I can probably hotwire it.'

'Well, do it,' Roxy said, and she looked at the cowboy with a look that, while hardly spelling trust, at least meant she was willing to consider other options to her standard "you're making all this bullshit up" line.

John C. hurried over to the vehicle. He was about to climb up into the driver's seat when he stopped, swore, then kicked the wheel.

'What's wrong?' Roxy asked.

'Tires are slit,' he said. 'He walked around the truck. 'All of them, even the spare.' He shook his head, looked over at Roxy. 'This thing ain't going nowhere. We're stuck out here.'

TWENTY SIX

Sam turned off his radio once he was in the car. He didn't need Edna nagging him about trivial nonsense that folks could sort out between themselves. He'd plenty of his own worries to be dealing with right now without the petty concerns of irate townsfolk.

He'd been drinking and probably should have called a cab. But pretty much every driver in town knew where he lived and most weren't interested in taking his fare. Many round these parts weren't registered. Hardly seemed worth pursuing, and Sam had no intention of doing so, but a nervous cabbie still made for an uncomfortable journey.

Sam took a right on Gillan Road, heading past the turnoff for town. The only lawyer who could see him today (and Sam had insisted on that) was a fellow by the name of Rogers. Worked out of an office just outside of town. Which suited Sam better: too many people would know his business if he went to one of the bigshots working out of the town centre. And hell, people knew enough of his business already...

Whitney's letter rested on the passenger seat. It was loose, flattened out as if laid on a table. He could read bits of it as he drove. He caught a glimpse of the proposed alimony and reiterated his disapproval. Five hundred dollars was quite a price to pay, considering how much she'd already made from him and their sham of a marriage.

He found the place and parked the car up along the sidewalk. Ignored the parking meter, knowing that no meter maid in her right mind would give the sheriff a ticket.

Sam opened the door to Hurst & Co. and stepped on in. He was greeted warmly by the secretary, some red haired thing with pale, freckled skin and a toothy grin. He was too old to know her and she was too young to care. He told her he had an appointment with a Mr Rogers and she told him to take a seat by reception. Sam did so reluctantly. He was keen to get into a private room before someone whom he *did* know wandered in.

Rogers was out to see him within two minutes. He looked painfully young, with a shiny face and hair that looked like it had been built on his head rather than grown there. He smelled like a salon. Dressed like one of those fags Sam would see on the box singing pop songs. He shook hands limply and then ushered Sam into his office.

'Got a letter from my wife,' Sam said before Rogers was even seated. He threw the damn thing across the desk. 'Bout a hearing they want me to attend. Happening in two weeks.'

Rogers cleared his throat. Pulled up a seat and started to read Whitney's letter.

'This is from another lawyer,' he highlighted as if that was news to Sam.

'Yep, Whitney's lawyer. What's this guy like, is he good? Old or young?'

Rogers just shrugged in response, looked to Sam and said, 'Sheriff Taylor, I don't even practise divorce cases.'

'Well, you're a lawyer,' Sam said. 'I'm guessing than means you've got some piece of paper somewhere that says you can give legal advice. Right?'

'Well…'

'So just tell me this: can she do this? Can she ask for this much money?'

'Sheriff Taylor—'

'Sam. Call me Sam.'

'Sam, I need you to know something,' Rogers began in a voice that sounded too tired and battleworn to come from such a young head. 'Alimony disputes are quite involved. They can stretch for some time. This is not my area of expertise but I wouldn't be able to answer your question even if it was. It's a matter of looking at income, expenditure, working out what can or can't be afforded and then—'

'Does it matter what I did to her?'

Rogers' brow furrowed. 'Excuse me?'

'These alimony disputes. Do they consider behaviour or is it just money-related?'

'Well, as I was saying, we would—'

'This woman has already ruined me, son. Not financially, I'll give her that, but every other damn way a woman could ruin a man, Whitney's done it. '

'I'm sorry, Sam. I don't get your meaning.'

'The news article!' Sam barked. Surely this guy wasn't *that* young that he didn't remember five years ago?

Sam remembered alright.

Even the title of the piece was clear in his mind: 'Living with the Law' it was called. And in it, Whitney picked every little scab from their twenty odd years together, smeared the darker days of their marriage across the paper for all to see. And, with her not drinking and him *very much* drinking, there was a lot that Sam read that was news even to him. It was news certainly to the townsfolk. In a place starved of 'real' celebrities to scrutinise and crucify, Sheriff Sam Taylor would do just fine.

'I'm sorry, Sam, I knew there was some trouble between yourself and Mrs Taylor in the past, but I'm not aware of the exact details. Yet as I've already said, I'm not best placed to handle this case. Maybe if I ask Susan, she can set up an appointment with our Divorce Attorney, Mr—'

'I hit her.' There, it was out. 'I hit her, son. Only the once, but I still hit her.' Sam ran a shaking hand through his silver hair. 'They didn't print that. They printed everything else, and hell there was enough even without it, but they left that out. Only now, when I read this letter, I'm left wondering if maybe they're going to bring it up in court. Screw me for more money.'

'Sheriff Taylor,' Rogers began, Sam noting how they were no longer on first name terms. 'I think we need to stop talking now. I think I need to make an appointment for you with my colleague who deals with cases like this, then let him handle things from hereon in.'

'It was just the once,' Sam said again. Tears filled his eyes as he spoke. 'Just that one time.' He looked up at Rogers. 'I'd been drinking, you see. And I guess I would have told someone before, maybe talked about it, but you know what this town's like. You even look at a damn woman funny and folks are saying Christie Keller's possessed you.'

The boy looked back at Sam with wide round eyes, like he hadn't a damn clue what Sam was talking about. And he probably didn't. Christie Keller was no more than a bogeyman to a kid that age. Something to scare him into going to bed early, or behaving himself around Christmas.

'Look, forget it,' Sam said, standing to his feet. 'Forget all of it, every word I told you.' He swiped the letter from Rogers' desk and made for the office door.

'Would you like me to—?'

'I'd like you to do nothing,' Sam said. 'Nothing, boy, do you hear me?'

'Yes sir.'

'Okay,' Sam said. 'Good.'

He left the office.

Back in the car, Sheriff Taylor couldn't hear himself think with all the shit rushing through his head. He needed a drink. He could hear those old demons from the past, telling him all sorts. He turned on the radio, hoping to drown the voices out.

And then he heard Edna's voice, nervous and strained.

'Sam? Where the hell have you been? Call came in. Looks like we've got a double homicide on our hands.'

TWENTY SEVEN

Nanna put the phone down, breathed a heavy sigh.

'Did you get him this time?' asked Gramps. He was cleaning the shotgun as he spoke.

'No, got his secretary. She told me she's already made that call to the city so somebody's coming. And I believe her. Edna Fox may be a gossip and a busy-body, but she's a woman of her word.'

Gramps made a wheezy noise, half-laugh, half-cough. 'State Police's no better than Sheriff Taylor. I ain't expecting nobody to come up here.' He inserted two fresh shells, snapped the barrels closed. 'But y'all ain't got nothin' to worry about. I ain't gonna let no murderous sum-bitches—'

'Paw!' Nanna scolded.

'—or Satanists or no dern ghost of Christie Keller, or whatever she's possessed this time, to get near you girls,' the old man continued, unabated. 'You hear?'

Nanna looked around the room, saw nothing in the girls' faces to suggest confidence.

'What about the cowboy?' she asked. 'You got that barn locked up tight?'

'Oh, he ain't going nowhere,' Gramps assured her.

A sudden gasp from Lori. 'The rooftop!' Everyone looked at her quizzically. 'Last night when I was in the barn with Char...' She stopped herself short, aware of Gramps' sudden scowl. 'Well, anyway, Gramps, you came in with the gun and we escaped through the rooftop and down a ladder.'

'Don't think I've forgotten about that,' the old man chided. 'We still need to have ourselves a conversation about that.'

Lori reddened.

Nanna stifled a smile.

'But you don't have to worry about no rooftop,' Gramps continued. 'I took away that ladder so unless the damn fool wants to break his legs, jumping, he ain't moving too far.'

'I don't think it's him,' Abby said.

Such a quiet girl, Nanna mused. Sitting there in the corner, hiding behind those spectacles of hers, all meek and mild. Sometimes you'd forget she was even there and that was a hard thing to do in a place this cramped.

Roxy was quick to counter: 'Oh come on, don't tell me you're buying all that BS about Christie Keller and the burlap man,' she laughed.

Nanna shushed Roxy, urged Abby to continue.

'I don't know what to believe,' she said. 'But there is something strange going on, I know that.' Abby sighed. 'Ever since Lori worked her...' she searched for the right words.

'Her magic,' Nanna said. Lori protested, but Nan shushed her too. 'This ain't no time for mincing words,' she said sternly. 'Magic's what you were calling on, girl. And magic's what you got.' She looked to Abby, her tone softening. 'Ain't that right, child?'

'I don't know how to describe it. But yes, there's something in the air since that time in the woods. And...'

'Speak your mind, girl,' Nanna urged.

Abby dropped her eyes, played with her hands. 'It's just that Christie Keller story. How folks viewed her after they took her to the lake.' She looked up, met Nanna's eyes. 'It ain't too different to how folks viewed me after I took care of Danny that time.'

Nanna swallowed hard. All the softness from before was gone from Abby's face and, in its place, was a darkness so unexpected that the old woman had to look away.

Lori placed her hand on Abby's, squeezed it.

'That Christie Keller story's just some old wives' tale for scaring kids,' she said. 'But what you did to Danny?' She smiled. 'Well, that shit made me *proud* of you, not scared.'

Abby's eyes misted up. 'It's just that…'

'What?'

'Well, it's just that what John said about seeing her on the lake…' she hesitated, sobbing. 'I saw her, too.'

'It was probably just an after-affect of the cleansing,' Lori said.

'I thought that, too,' Abby whimpered. 'First I thought I was seeing things. But when I looked again, she was still there.'

'When was this?' Roxy asked.

'The night we got here,' Abby said. 'You guys had gone to bed, but I couldn't sleep. I was standing by the lake when I saw her. It was just like John said; how she kept reappearing in different places.' She paused again, emotion welling. 'What if she… What if Christie Keller brought Danny back somehow?' she said, and then she broke down crying.

Lori placed a hand on the back of Abby's head and held her close. Abby let loose into her friend's shoulder.

'It's okay,' Lori said, caressing Abby's head from the top, down. She looked up and made a face at the others in the room. *Just give us a minute.*

Roxy let out an exasperated sigh and stormed up the stairs. Seconds later a door slammed on the second floor.

Nanna shook her head and tutted at Roxy's rudeness. She pulled herself out of her chair and walked to the window, suddenly feeling the urge to move. The tension from before was even worse now, spreading around the room like gas.

She opened the door to get some air, stepped onto the porch.

The sun was in its prime, the sky crayon blue. The trees seemed closer, as if the woods were closing in on the small cabin.

Nanna found her hanky and wiped her brow, suddenly sweating.

Her eyes found the porch swing and widened.

'What the—?' she breathed.

Nanna hurried over to the porch and found the burlap man was back, slumped on his swing as always.

But something was different…

Her eyes went right to his empty left hand. At his feet lay a clutch of wilted flowers. Magnolias, azaleas, wild iris, and Cajun hibiscus, it looked like. Nanna went to pick them up but was distracted by the little red speckles that covered the burlap man's clothes and his dome face.

It looked like blood.

TWENTY EIGHT

As he pulled onto the trek, leading to the old Sawyer cabin by the woods, Sam felt the thirst hit him. Maybe it was the smell of damp wood, the condensation heavy like mist on those trees causing moss to coat each bark like fur. Whatever the reason, Sam Taylor needed a drink. Something to steady himself, take away the shakes.

A goddamn double homicide, he mused, unscrewing the cap of his pint, swigging then replacing it. Black Water had known some trouble over the years, but a double homicide was bad even by this town's standards. Last time Sam had seen something like this was 1963, back when he was a rookie. The sheriff at the time had sent him up to the scene and he remembered finding the bodies of two men by the lake. Everyone and their dog was talking about it, some saying it were Christie Keller's work. But the real story, of course, proved altogether more frightening: the two men were black as the waters themselves. And this was the work of the Klan.

The sheriff at the time was a man called Wight, as church-going as men were back in those days, and not adverse to hatin' on "niggers" from time to time. But this was an insult to him.

They pull this shit in my town? he seethed. *No gaddam way.*

So he worked the case like a man possessed, finally arresting two local businessmen for murder. But a hung jury got the whole thing thrown out of court and the two men walked free, heroes to some folks.

Those men were still around today. Older now, infirm. They used to drink in the bar and Tom would laugh and joke with them like he did with all the men. But Sam could never as much as look them in the eye. The whole thing had left a real dirty taste in his mouth.

As he drove, he wondered what could have happened up here now. The lake had history, for sure, and rumours abounded about nefarious things having gone down in those woods. Until these recent sightings, Christie Keller had been relegated to stories passed among the local teens, left-over hippies, and fringe-dwellers of various persuasions. Now everyone and their uncle had an opinion on the authenticity (or lack thereof) of the legend, which was both revered and scoffed at in the town of Black Water and on the woods and lake that bore its name.

The Stogies were supposed to reinvent the area. They were supposed to restore respectability and bring jobs. But eighty-five percent of the employees were outsourced and respectability came with morbid curiosity and big, dumb, mostly Yankee smiles on big, dumb, mostly Yankee faces hoping to experience an honest-to-goodness Southern-fried haunting. The Stogies had become their lighthouse beacon.

Not that Sam gave a shit. Live and let live was his motto. And that's exactly what he told those evangelicals in town. *Protest all you like,* he said. *But I hear of one of you men stepping over the line and doing something more than waving placards, I'll hit your ass with everything the law has.*

He had given ol' man Sawyer a similar warning. The blind old coot had been known to chase away curious folks with that shotgun of his. Until Sam put a stop to it, hitting a few of them with fines, people were making the five mile trek from the Stogie's to visit the scene of Christie Keller's infamous drowning at least once a week.

I don't like it any more than you do, he'd said to the old man, *but you pull that trigger on one a those folks and I'll haul you in faster'n you can spit. Ya hear?*

Sam had an uneasy suspicion that he was looking at that very scenario right now, and he shuddered at the thought of having to live up to his word and haul in an old blind man like that. He knew the old timer wouldn't go easy. And his wife would sure as shit have something to say about it. Then there was the paperwork. So much paperwork.

Stupid old fool, Sam thought, more frustrated than angry. *I warned you!*

He pulled up to the clearing and killed the engine. Peered out at the old car he'd parked beside. It was real messed up, with some graffiti scrawled in red paint.

'NO ESCAPE' Sam read.

He tutted. Maybe it weren't the old man after all. *What the hell's been going on up here?*

Sam crept up the path out of the clearing and towards the cabin on stealth, intent on surveying the scene before anyone knew he'd arrived. He moved out from the woods and into the open plain, sneaking another swig from his pint while he sized up the old cabin coming into view. It looked small and rustic and creepy as fuck. Same as always.

The old Sawyer place was a fixture of these parts and had been as far back as Sam could remember. He hated coming here, even as a teenager, when he and his friends would dare each other to knock on the door. Sam was the

163

most adventurous of all them and yet he never got too far beyond the tree-line before he reckoned that thing on the porch could see him.

Sam's eyes scanned the barn next door, and then back to the cabin.

He clocked the old burlap man on the porch swing again and shook his head. So many sleepless nights wasted on Ol' Geordi. And yet, now, he couldn't shake the same uneasiness that he felt back then.

He slid the burlap man a look as he approached the cabin. *I'm not afraid of you.* He looked away... and immediately whipped his head back toward the porch swing. The burlap man, who he could've sworn just moved, was still slumped on top of it.

Sam blinked, then looked again. Then took a long swig from his pint.

You should be ashamed of yourself, he mused. *An officer of the law still afraid of the bogeyman. You've dealt with real criminals with real weapons capable of maiming or killing. It didn't move. Just a trick of the light. Same as when you were a kid.*

That wasn't entirely true, but it was enough to calm his nerves.

He slipped the pint back into his pocket.

The same trick of light had befallen anyone who ventured too close to the Sawyer cabin over the years. The mailman. The Black Water Code Inspector. Various salesmen. The local teens.

Sam took another step towards the cabin when he heard a voice.

'Hey! Over here!'

Sam spun toward the sound, his hand finding the handle of his holstered revolver. The voice had come from the barn.

One hand still on the revolver, Sam looked to the cabin and the burlap man before gingerly moving towards the barn. He reached the doors, found a rusty old padlock and chain threaded through the door handles, locking the old place up nice and tight.

He noticed a gap in the wood, went to peer through, when an eye appeared suddenly at the other side causing Sam to simultaneously jump and draw his weapon.

'Jesus,' Sam breathed, lowering his revolver and pressing one hand to his chest.

'Help me!' the eye said. 'Those crazy old negroes gone and locked me in here.'

The voice was male, young. Very Southern.

'And what you done for them to go and do a thing like that?' Sam asked, sliding the revolver back into the holster at his hip. Despite all the Voodoo bullshit, and the old man's occasional run ins, the Sawyers were peaceful, decent folks. A little strange, maybe, but not the type to lock someone in a barn without provocation.

'I done nothing. I swear it, man.'

'He's done something, alright,' another voice said, causing Sam to swing around. The old timer held a shotgun but it was uncocked and bent over his arm. 'We just ain't sure whether it's murder.'

'Was it you who called it in?'

The old man sniffed, spat on the ground. 'Was my wife. Tell you the truth, Sheriff Taylor, I wouldn't be inclined to call the law here for much. No offence.'

'None taken.' Sam looked to the cabin. 'Your wife in there?'

'That she is.'

'Well, I'll need to speak with her if that's okay with you, sir.'

'What about me?' the voice from the barn called. 'Don't leave me here! PLEASE!'

Sam didn't turn, instead raising an eyebrow at the old man and saying, 'He can wait.'

TWENTY NINE

Those bitches!

He'd skin them alive. He'd skin that nigger-loving cop, too. He'd skin every last one of them.

John C. Lane paced the length and breadth of the old barn, head full of expletives and revenge fantasies. Truth of the matter was that he was royally fucked. The old barn was locked up tight.

No escape.

Charlie's rich pop would leave no stone unturned in bringing his boy's killer to justice. Those big city lawyers would surely uncover John C.'s history with the Baton Rouge PD. Criminal Harassment and Unlawful Entry were the charges. His ex-girlfriend Clara the victim. He didn't reckon she saw him following her around for weeks, thought he'd covered his tracks when he broke into her house that night. The Judge gave John C. a scolding before the verdict was read aloud: some bullshit about controlling his anger and learning how to treat women. Blah. Blah. Blah. They found him guilty and sentenced him to thirty days in the county lock up and six months of Anger Management.

John C. considered himself lucky. It would've been much worse had they known about the knife clipped to his belt that night, or that he'd been hoping to find Clara and her new man in bed together. Maybe he'd have never actually done anything.

But sometimes he wondered.

Anger and violence generally went hand in hand in John C.'s bloodline...

Either way, once those big city lawyers heard that bitch Roxy's testimony, they would use the whole Clara incident to show prior history. They would lock him up and throw away the key. And all because of that *FUCKING BITCH!*

John C. continued to pace, continued to fixate on his probable fate. Guilty of murder. Prison. Death Row. He saw Roxy's face twisted in anger, hurling blame, calling him names.

He pushed aside any images of Charlie and Jake and of that witch, Christie Keller. Nobody would believe him. They'd laugh at him when he brought up the burlap man, all those weird words and symbols moving around his burlap face and head as he stabbed his buddies to death with that cane knife.

John C. began to sweat. He balled his fists and snaked his neck. He wanted to punch something, hurrying over to the nearest wall and cocking his fist back. But something stopped him from following through.

He wiped the sweat from his eyes, squinted against the slivers of sun piercing through the spaces in the wood. One of the planks was slightly bowed away from the foundation. It looked like water damage, extending all the way to the bottom of the plank on one side right through to the next plank over.

John worked at the bowed area. The wood was near rotten and threatening to give, but the spaces between the planks were too narrow for his fingers to fit through.

He scanned the barn, looking for something that he could use to wedge between the planks, noticing an old pitchfork on the ground and picking it up. He weighed it in his hands, looked at the walls, and ultimately decided that it wouldn't work.

He threw down the pitchfork and continued to search the barn. Nothing else jumped out at him. He spotted an old crate and sat himself down to think things through.

Maybe if I ...

His ass went right through the crate. John C Lane cried out in shock. But there was something underneath him, something the crate was holding.

Tools.

He ruffled through the crate's contents, found a rusty old crowbar and fished it out. This would do. Then he noticed something else inside: a knife.

He lifted the knife, ran his finger along the blade then slid it under his belt.

He found the crowbar again then returned to the water-damaged planks and ran his finger over the rotting wood.

This won't take long at all, he mused.

THIRTY

'Law's here,' the old man announced as he pushed open the door.

Nanna was in the kitchen area, three girls gathered at the table.

Sam entered the cabin and tipped his hat to her.

'Ma'am,' he said.

She nodded. 'Sheriff.'

Sam shuffled coyly over to the table, placed his hands on one of the chairs and asked, 'May I?'

'You may.' Nanna waited until he sat down. 'I'd offer you a drink,' she said, her eyes fixed on his, 'but I know you're on duty.'

The comment was loaded, but Sam didn't turn it. 'A glass of water would be fine,' he said.

Nanna fixed him his water and passed it to him. 'That secretary of yours…'

'Yes, Edna.'

'That's the one. She told me she'd put a call in to the city.'

'That's correct. But then she got me. I called them again, told them I could take care of things.'

'And can you, Sheriff?'

'Sorry?'

'Take care of things.'

Another loaded comment. Word spread fast

round these parts, it seemed. Sam shuffled in his chair, cleared his throat. 'Well, that remains to be seen, ma'am, don't it?'

Nanna smiled thinly.

From his jacket, Sam drew a notepad and pen. Scribbled something to test the pen then looked to Nanna. 'So tell me about this call you made. I'm led to believe there's been a double homicide. Can you tell me where I can find, er, the victims' bodies?'

'No I cannot.'

The sheriff's eyes narrowed.

'Well, what about the call you made? You must have had reason...'

'That young man out in the barn came to the house last night, screaming and crying about murder in the woods.'

Sam's eyebrows rose.

'And all I know is that his hands and shirt were bloody and he'd supposedly done a number on my Lori's car.' Nanna looked to one of the girls, a pretty young thing with black features and white skin. The girl nodded agreement, and Nanna continued. 'Well, Lori's Gramps and young Roxy here,' another nod to a second girl, this one blonde and slim, 'went out to the boy's camp, found more blood and their stuff all trashed. The boy says his buddies were killed, but not by human hands, no. He swears it's the work of Christie Keller and our burlap man.'

Sam laughed. The sound rang out hollow in the cabin. He felt aware of himself, noticed his hand was shaking and Nanna's eyes fall upon it. Pulled it under the table. 'Christie Keller, you say?'

'And our burlap man. But I ain't saying nothing,' Nanna corrected him. 'I'm just telling you like it was told to me.'

Sam breathed a sigh. He looked to the young mixed-race girl.

'Your car that old Volkswagen in the clearing down there?'

'Yes it is,' she said.

Sam nodded. 'Okay, well, guess I'd better talk to the young man in the barn then,' he said.

A sudden noise like wood shattering. It came from outside.

'Stay here!' Sam said, reaching for his revolver.

THIRTY ONE

It had been a long time since Sheriff Sam Taylor had even drawn his gun, never mind fired the damn thing. And with his hands shaking like they were now, his aim wouldn't be worth shit.

He moved past the burlap man on the porch, eyes sweeping across to the barn.

Near its doors, he found a small pile of broken wood. He spotted the redneck, sprinting off into the woods, thought of firing, thought better of it and lowered his gun.

The old man followed Sam out onto the porch, shotgun in hand.

'Too late,' Sam said. 'He's gone. I'll put a call into town, have him picked up if he heads back there.'

'He won't get that far.'

'He must have a car or something. How else did he get here?'

'They had a truck. But someone, maybe he himself, did a number on it.'

Sam looked to the trees, thought on that a moment. *Why would he do that? Cripple himself like that.*

'I'd like to take a look for myself. Can someone take me there?'

The old man sighed. 'I'd take you there myself. Sure, I can't see for shit, but I know my way around these woods.' He tapped his head. 'Got it all mapped out here. But truth of the matter is that someone needs to stay here, protect the women.'

Sam nodded respectfully, although he had his doubts as to just how much protection a shotgun wielding old blind man could offer those women.

'I'll take you,' another voice piped up.

Sam turned round, found the blonde girl standing by the porch swing where the old burlap man rested. He looked her up and down.

'What's your name, darling?'

'Roxy Blue. And I know where those boys were camping and where that truck of theirs is parked. The tires are slashed, like Gramps says, and there's a lotta blood. But I still think that redneck's lying, that his buddies are waiting out there and have ideas on us.'

'Maybe you should call for help,' the old man suggested.

Sam Taylor's face burned red. He was tired of the loaded comments. Tired of the remarks and the sniggers wherever he went. Tired of people questioning his ability to effectively police this backwoods borough. But what was he going to do; shoot the old man and his wife, and everyone else in town, save for Edna?

'I don't need no help to deal with a coupla knuckle-draggin' pranksters,' he shot back before turning to Roxy. 'I'd say you're right, Miss. That this is all just some elaborate prank cooked up by him and his buddies. But they've messed with the wrong guy today. That's fer *damn* sure.'

Roxy grinned. 'Preach it, Sheriff!'

'Come on if you're coming,' Sam told her, his voice still irritable.

'Wait, can I come too?'

Sam Taylor turned around, regarded the girl who had spoken. She was a mousey sort, built like a piece of string, a pair of wireframe glasses parked on her nose.

'Sure, why not,' he said morosely. 'More the merrier.'

From behind some foliage, John C. Lane watched as the group went their separate ways, the old folks and their little witch back to the cabin, the lawman and the other two girls off towards the river.

He waited several minutes before exiting the woods and moving towards his target.

THIRTY TWO

Sam Taylor looked to Abby, clearly trying to make conversation. 'So, what were you girls doing out here anyway?'

Abby looked nervously to Roxy, who answered for her, 'Just chilling.'

'Chilling, eh?' The sheriff regarded her suspiciously. 'Dangerous place to chill. Don't you know the history of these woods?'

Roxy laughed, shook her head. 'Don't *you* start with that Christie Keller BS.'

'*Please,*' he scoffed. 'I'm talking about homicide. Real life stuff. These woods have seen their fair share over the years. And that lake where you girls were *chilling*? Well, that's where the bodies usually end up.'

'Well, you sure know how to sweet talk a girl,' Roxy said with a wink.

But Sam remained serious. 'That's the trouble with young folks today,' he complained. 'No common sense. Always heading off on their own to some cabin in the woods, lying to their parents, never telling anyone where they've gone.'

Roxy's eyes narrowed. 'Think we're a bit old for the Scooby Doo lecture, Sheriff. And ain't you a bit young to be giving it?'

He smiled and in that moment, Roxy felt her heart skip. Sam Taylor was no spring chicken, despite what she'd just told him, and the years could have been kinder to his pockmarked face and creased eyes. But there was a handsome man buried somewhere beneath that smile.

'The campsite. It's just up here,' she said, glad of the distraction.

They found the guys' campsite as before. The metal spit arched over the memory of a fire in the center, the tent right beside it, the open flap revealing a couple of empty sleeping bags garnished with porno mags. Swatches of dead foliage and formless shrubs tore a path through the camp; desiccated tree roots protruding from the earth, twisting into painful shapes.

Sam spotted something on the trees and ran his finger over it. Blood. It had hardened from the Louisiana breeze coming off the lake, given time to mature into something rightly funky. Sam narrowed his eyes and looked around the camp.

He spotted the pickup, parked nearby. Its tires were flat, just like Roxy had told him, the foliage at its wheels looking like it had been scorched or something. He noticed blood smeared on the hood and what seemed to be the path of a body being dragged away.

'It's probably deer's blood,' Roxy said, her tone dismissive.

But Sam was still lost in thought, hands on his hunkers as he stood looking the vehicle over. His jacket was peeled back revealing the badge and gun on his belt.

Black Water was no New Orleans, but Sam had seen enough to know what the scene of a violent crime looked and smelled like.

'I'll say this for them guys: if they have staged this whole scene, like you say,' he pursed his lips, 'well, they've done a good job of it.' He pointed at the hood. 'See this dent?'

Roxy looked, thought nothing of it.

'The size and shape is consistent with an average-sized man being thrown up onto it.' He bent over, pulled something from the truck's grill, held it up for Roxy to see. 'And this here is *human* hair, not deer.' He pointed out several areas where the dirt and shrubs and the low-reaching branches had been disturbed and said, 'You see that? There. There. And there. Looks, to me like a violent tussle took place. And that smell? It's the smell of death. Something you never for—'

A shotgun blast in the distance startled them.

Roxy looked to Abby. The other girl looked scared.

'I-I think it came from over there.' She pointed one shaking hand.

'The Sawyer place,' Sam said. He drew his revolver. 'Stay close to me.'

They hurried back towards the cabin.

Twenty minutes ago…

'What if what John's saying is true?' Lori said as she stood by the window eagle-eyeing the barrier of oak trees that bordered the woods proper. 'If something happens to them, it's all my fault.'

'Ain't nothin' gonna happen to them, child,' Nanna said. She stood in the kitchen, waiting for the tea kettle to whistle. 'Now git on away from that windah.'

Gramps was seated in his favorite chair facing forward like some old wax dummy. His eyes were hidden behind the lenses of his glasses. The shotgun lay across his lap, old, weathered hands resting on top. The old man had been known to fall asleep that way. There was some question as to whether or not he was asleep right now.

'How can you be so sure?' Lori replied. 'I mean, shouldn't we be figuring out a way to stop it, just in case?'

'You seem to have the supernatural world all figured out,' Nanna sniped. 'Why don't you tell us?'

'I'm serious, Nanna.'

'No. What you are is naïve.'

'Umm Hmm,' Gramps agreed, putting to rest any question that he was asleep.

'And feeling guilty,' Nanna added. 'As you should. Now, it's true you stirred something up, but like I said before, it ain't no Christie Keller. What you done is more like...' She thought for a moment. 'More like a foot kickin' up sediment in the shallow water, is all. Now stop all that frettin' and carryin' on, and git away from that windah. Ain't nothin' you can do til they come back anyhow.'

Lori rolled her eyes, blew out some air. She moved away from the window under protest and stood there with her arms folded over her chest like a defiant child.

'I told you, Lori, you had—'

'No business foolin' with things you don't understand,' Lori mocked, talking over Nanna.

'You watch yourself, young lady,' Gramps came alive and said.

Nanna glared at her granddaughter, taken aback by the girl's insubordination, but also pitying her somewhat. Girl was only trying to help a friend, after all. They had raised her to be thoughtful of others, to treat people the way she wanted to be treated.

'Come now, child,' the old woman began in a softened voice, 'I know you meant well. That you were only trying to help your dear Abby. But as the saying goes, "Hell is paved with good intentions."'

'They do say that don't they,' Gramps quipped, deadfaced.

Lori stormed upstairs in a huff. A door slammed shortly after she reached the second floor.

A few seconds passed.

'If slamming doors was a talent, these youngins would be a shoe-in for the Ivy Leagues,' the old man said without moving a muscle.

'Why'd you have to go instigatin' things?' Nanna scolded.

'Cause I couldn't think straight with all that yappin'.'

Nanna's eyes narrowed as she looked on her husband, 'I'll show you yappin',' she said with a raised fist.

'Umm Hmm,' the old man replied.

His mind was elsewhere. Focused on some ill-advised mission to guard Nanna and Lori at all cost. It made the old woman smile.

The tea kettle whistled. Nanna turned off the stove, filled two waiting cups and let the water sift through the tea bags floating inside.

'You think they caught 'em?' she turned to her husband and said.

The old man thought for a moment, said, 'This is Sam Taylor we're talking about.'

Good point.

When the tea was ready, Nanna used a spoon to strain the excess fluid from the tea-bags and tossed them in the trash. She liked her tea plain. Gramps liked his heavy on the honey and with lemon. She prepared it just the way he liked it, walked over and placed the steaming cup under his nose.

'Smells good,' the old man said.

He took the cup, and lifted it to his mouth, puckering his lips, anticipating the hot liquid against his skin.

Nanna stood over him awaiting his approval. It came by way of a satisfied nod. The old man's posture relaxed.

'You sure do know what I like,' he said.

More than that she knew what it took to calm him down. Thirty years ago it was sex, a good meal, or a few swigs of her sister's moonshine. That was all anyone could take of that shit. Nowadays all it took was a cup of tea, heavy on the honey and with lemon.

Nanna grabbed her cup and made for the door.

'Where do you think you're going?' Gramps said.

Nanna stopped, turned to her husband. 'Just out to the porch. Do I have your permission?'

She didn't wait for him to answer before heading out the door.

She padded out onto the porch and stood at the edge of the steps. Took a deep, cleansing breath. A memory struck her as she exhaled. She lowered the cup and turned. Her eyes found the wilted flowers lying at Geordi's feet, the ones she meant to pick up earlier.

Nanna walked over and, holding onto the porch railing, crouched beside the burlap man. Her knees weren't what they used to be. She set her cup down on the porch and gathered the wilted flowers together in a clutch, careful not to damage the brittle stems. She placed them in Geordi's left hand. It took a couple of tries before she got his hand to remain closed.

'There. Good as new,' she said when she was done.

Nanna looked up. Her eyes landed on Geordi's burlap dome, right where his eyes would be if he had any. But there were only Creole incantations and West African glyphs scribbled in red. Her head fell to a tilt as she looked on her burlap guardian with affection. At this point Geordi was like a member of the family.

'You wouldn't know anything about what's going on here, now, would you?' she joked.

Nanna used the railing to stand, retrieving her cup on the way. She walked back over to the edge of the steps. Picking up where she left off, she inhaled a deep whiff of Louisiana air and blew it out, expelling all the bad vibes that had gathered in her chest since all this business had started. She took comfort in the view laid out before her. The open field. The wall of oak trees. The uneven ceiling of green. The sky seemingly set on top.

Her eyes grazed the sun and she raised a hand to shade them. And there she stood, speculating and waiting to hear the sound of approaching voices.

Nanna felt a sudden presence over her left shoulder and, in an instant, the sun's warmth was replaced by an icy anxiety. There was a momentary chill in the air. The hairs on her arm stood on end.

Nanna spun around and right into the vice-like grip of a gloved hand. It clamped over her throat and squeezed a choking whimper from her.

She felt her feet leave the ground.

Her bulging eyes found the owner of the gloved hand. Geordi, the burlap man. Nanna dangled from the end of his outstretched arm, kicking and flailing and struggling to breathe.

Geordi flipped the cane knife in his other hand and planted the tip of the blade into the wall next to him. Then he pulled what was left of the magnolias, azaleas, wild iris, and Cajun hibiscus from the pocket of his P-coat and shoved them into Nanna's mouth.

The burlap man's hand continued to squeeze. The crushed flowers fell from Nanna's mouth. Her kicking and flailing became less aggressive and she began wheezing involuntarily. Her eyes rolled back.

Geordi snatched the knife from the wall and cocked his arm back.

'You take your filthy hands offa her or I'll blow your head inta next Tues-dee,' came a voice from behind.

Gramps stood firm in the doorway, shotgun

in hand. The weapon was aimed squarely at the back of Geordi's head. Nanna went to cry out to the old man but consciousness escaped her.

Geordi hesitated, his head half-turning to the left. Nanna dangled limp from his out-stretched arm.

Gramps tracked the burlap man with the gun, ear tuned to his every move. His finger curled around the trigger. 'I *SAID*...'

With his arm outstretched, Geordi simply opened his hand. Nanna dropped to the porch steps and tumbled down them all limbs and joints rolling. Gramps followed her descent with concern, hearing every last meeting of skin and bone against the hard edged wood.

'Ma?' he called out to her.

The burlap man swung around, leading with the cane knife. The blade connected with the shotgun's long barrel and knocked the thing from the old man's hands.

Next Geordi thrust an opened palm at Gramp's shoulder, shoving the old man back-ward and off his feet.

Gramps landed on the living room floor and cried out in pain. Something snapped in his right arm.

Geordi's silhouette darkened the doorway. He seemed hesitant to walk through it, but ulti-mately did so. Gramps lifted himself to a seated position, coughing and wincing as the burlap man reached for him.

'Ma?' he called out in desperation, craning his neck and listening for a response of some kind. 'You okay, Ma?'

The burlap man turned his head toward the

door waiting, along with the old man, for a response. When none came, he turned back to Gramps and shook his head, 'no.'

Gramps struggled against Geordi's hold. He wrapped one hand around the grigri bag dangling from his neck and lifted himself to a defiant stand. His glasses fell from his face, exposing milk white eyes.

'I've lived through the Jim Crow South, the Germans, the Japs, and good old boys that would make you shit yer britches,' the old man raged. 'So, I ain't afraid-a-you, whoever you are!'

Geordi's posture inflated, as if enraged by Gramps' defiance. He pulled the old man closer.

Gramps spat at the flat burlap face.

Geordi brought the blade up under the old man's chin and pushed the tip against his skin forcing his head back.

'I'll see you on the other side,' the old man groaned as the tip of the blade pierced his skin, a stream of blood racing down the shiny surface toward the hilt.

Geordi kept his face close as he turned, and twisted, and pushed upward on the handle eliciting cries of pain from the old man. More blood.

There was a loud boom from behind. The sound shook the floor of the cabin.

The turning, and twisting, and pushing suddenly stopped. Geordi yanked the blade out and let go of the handle. The knife fell from his hand and impaled by the tip in the wooden cabin floor. His arms and legs flew out to the side and he became instantly rigid. He bucked to a jolt surging through his entire body. Without warning, the burlap man was snatched upward by some invisible force and made to hover more than a foot off the floor.

Gramps slapped his hand over the wound underneath his chin and turned his ear toward the door.

'That you, Ma?' he said in an optimistic voice.

Indeed it was.

Nanna lay partially on her stomach just outside the front door. Her hair was dishevelled, clothing torn, her face and arms scratched and bleeding. Her eyes had gone true white. Witchy glow.

She sat raised up on one arm chanting in Creole. The other arm was extended toward the burlap man, brandishing her hand like a weapon, fingers flexed and spread apart.

The doorframe had been badly damaged by whatever she had done. It looked like a hurricane had blown through the small space and caused it to buckle inward. The chewed and broken wood shrieked and whined. The front door hung on by a single hinge.

Nanna dragged herself forward with one arm. She kept the other arm held out in front of her like some spiritual antennae. She stopped midway through the doorway and called out in a strained voice, 'I'm here.'

Nanna glared up at the burlap man, hovering Christ-like in her living room, said, 'How dare you bring your evil into my home! How *DARE* you!'

She looked to her right and back. There was a sliding sound from the porch. Seconds later Gramps' shotgun floated through the doorway on invisible strings. Guided by Nanna's eyes, the weapon floated up to the burlap man. The tip of the barrel pressed against the back of his head.

'Now, let's end this foolishness once and for all, Mister *John C. Lane.*'

Gramps laughed heartily. Blood ran down his neck from the wound underneath his chin, but, at the moment, he couldn't give two shits about that. The old man got a thrill from seeing his wife go all Voodoo Queen on this fool. It had been so long that he almost forgot just how gleefully excited it made him.

He pointed at the floating burlap assassin and said in a nearly incoherent collection of syllables, 'Y...you gon get it now, son...'

Bewitched, the burlap man reached both arms up, placed his hands at either side of the burlap dome and began to lift it off his head.

Gramps continued to laugh and point.

Just then, the doorframe collapsed and rained splintered wooden chunks down on top of Nanna. The roof buckled. More wood fell, landing on Nanna's head, crushing her skull.

Gramps stopped laughing, yelled, 'Ma! No!'

The burlap man dropped to the floor, suddenly free of the invisible force that held him afloat. The shotgun jerked, and fired off a round at the ceiling upon its release, releasing more wood.

Geordi landed in a crouch at the old man's feet. Gramps was in shock, his face fixed in a horrified expression.

Shaking off a dizzy spell, the burlap man snatched the cane knife from the floor, flipped it in his hand, and swung it at an upward arc towards Gramps groin as he simultaneously sprung to his feet. The blade caught the old man in the crease between his scrotum and thigh and bit clean through to his abdomen. A deep barking sound leapt from his mouth. His face tightened. Groaning through clenched teeth, the old man's hands immediately found the knife handle and pushed against Geordi's thrust to no avail. His cries dampened, those milky white eyes bulging wider than seemed possible.

Geordi pulled the blade out, flipping it downward to shake off the excess blood.

Gramps placed shaking hands over the leaking wound in his groin. His face riddled with pain, his mouth falling open in hang-jawed horror. Blood drooled over his lip and oozed to the floor.

The old man staggered sideways. His foot slipped on the pool of blood forming, giving way from under him, and he fell into a split, tearing the wound open further.

Gramps watched in horror as his bowels poured from the wound and collected on the floor in a steaming pile that was still attached by a plump, moist tentacle of large-intestine reaching up inside him.

His head fell back. His milky white eyes rolled around the sockets. At one point they locked onto the burlap man, who just stood there watching him.

Geordi raised one hand and sent Gramps off with a tight-fingered wave meant to mock his plight. Then he lifted one foot, placed the sole of his shoe against the old man's chest, and shoved him backward with disdain.

As Gramps lay there, quickly fading from existence, he thought he heard someone scream. It sounded both male and female, both close up and far away. At this point he couldn't tell.

THIRTY THREE

Sam Taylor sprinted toward the cabin porch, watching as John C. Lane hurled wild fists at Lori, like he were fighting an opponent three times his size. One of those wild fists connected with the side of the girl's head. Sam winced at the crack of knuckles against skull.

The blow appeared to daze the girl and she collapsed on the stairs.

John C. attempted to straddle her.

As Lori flailed, and kicked, and clawed, and scratched, John C. switched between trying to control her wrists and raining down more punches of his own.

Roxy was a few strides behind Sam, having just cleared the barrier of trees, where Abby still stood, horrified.

'He's gonna kill her,' Roxy screamed.

Her voice reached Sam, who was still shocked by the brutality that unfolded before him. He thought suddenly of Whitney, how he'd been guilty of striking a woman himself, and a burning stab of guilt entered his chest.

Sam dropped into a stance, took aim, and yelled at John C's back.

'FREEZE!'

But John C. had other plans. He wrapped a hand around Lori's throat and squeezed until she made a choking sound. Then he stiffened his arm, pinning her to the steps.

Lori squirmed, and flailed, and kicked, and scratched.

'I said FREEZE!'

With his other hand, John C. reached for something on the porch. He lifted that something into view. It was Geordi's cane knife.

'Just shoot him!' Roxy cried.

But Sam waited, determined to give the young cowboy every opportunity to down tools. He had pulled his gun several times throughout his career. Even fired a few warning shots. But he never had to use deadly force. The idea of killing another man seemed far less appealing than it had when he played it out in his head.

'Don't do it, son!' he warned, but John C.'s arm continued on its upward trajectory. The knife-blade gleamed in the sunlight.

'The hell are you waiting for?!' Roxy yelled at Sam, 'Just shoot him for Christ Sakes!'

'This is your last warning—' Sam started to say when Roxy ran up and attempted to snatch the gun away from him. He shoved her aside and immediately refocused his aim on John C just as the blade reached the apex of its upward climb and began its descent.

Sam squeezed off two shots quickly.

He heard Roxy gasp.

Abby let loose a bloodcurdling scream.

A brief silence followed.

Sam relaxed his aim and watched as John C. Lane struggled to stand. The cowboy made a sound like prolonged surprise, like he was trying to catch his breath. He was bleeding from the back of his head. Another stain formed on his upper back. Sam tracked the young cowboy with his gun as he staggered forwards, all the while reaching up and palming the side of his head as if to hold it together.

His eyes found Sam, the left eye peeking through a mask of blood that painted half his face red. Sam noticed that the young man's eyes were blue. It was a fleeting observation.

The blood poured from a large, venous welt with a fissure down the middle where one bullet, after having entered through the back of John C.'s head, had tried, unsuccessfully to exit above his left eyebrow. The blunted tip of the spent slug poked through the fissure.

John C.'s face tightened into a painful grimace. Staggering forward, he reached out to Sam. He stopped and wobbled loose-legged, and then seemed to concentrate in order to remain standing. He squeezed his eyes shut and groaned at a surge of pain, and then opened them wide as dinner plates.

Sam felt the fear in those eyes and he wanted no part of it. He lowered his gun, and backed away from John C., whose eyes pleaded with him to stay.

John C. staggered forward again and Sam back-stepped. His mouth was moving, trying to form words, but only sounds fell out.

'Mah... Mah... Mah...,' he said.

Sam looked over at Roxy, who appeared similarly stupefied. He looked behind him and found Abby lying in the grass where she had apparently fainted.

'Lori, NO!' Roxy screamed.

Sam whipped around in time to see Lori run up behind John C. wielding the cane knife in a two-handed grip. She lifted it up over her head, a feral scowl peeking through her raised arms, and grunted from deep in her gut as she brought it down on John C.'s head.

Sam turned away at the last minute. He didn't think to cover his ears, and heard the meeting of blade, skull, and soft, grey matter clear as crystal.

He turned and saw John C.'s lifeless body laid out flat at Lori's feet. He looked like a break dancer stuck in some awkward transitional pose. The cane knife had cut right down the middle of the cowboy's face. His head was turned to the side, the knife's long handle sticking out the back.

Lori stood over him, badly beaten and breathing heavily. Yet she seemed strangely calm. Her head hung low, her battered face hidden behind ringlets of hair dampened with sweat.

Sam and Roxy looked at each other. Their faces bore the weight of what they had just witnessed. Abby was still flat out in the grass.

'Lori?' Roxy called out in a gentle tone. 'You okay?'

Sam made a face at Roxy's question. *Of course she's not okay.*

Roxy moved gingerly towards her friend.

'You did what you had to do, Lori. It was either you or him. There's nothing to feel guilty about.'

Lori's eyes rolled up and peered through her hair. Her left eye was badly swollen. Her lip was busted. Blood poured from a broken nose.

She shook her head, 'No.'

Tears streamed down her battered face.

'It's okay,' Sam assured. 'You're gonna be okay. Let's just get you to a hospital.'

It looked like Lori was about to say something, but then her eyes rolled back and she crumbled to the grass like an imploded skyscraper. Roxy attempted to catch her, but arrived seconds too late.

'Just relax,' Danny whispered in Abby's ear.

She flinched at the moisture from his hot breath.

'I'm scared,' she whimpered.

'Just go with it.'

She had said *NO* so many times, but Danny kept pushing. "Let me tie you up. It'll be a blast. You'll see."

She wanted to trust him, to let go and give Danny complete control. She knew that's what he wanted, maybe what he needed. Like an addict needs their drug. And Abby being a pleaser.

Abby lay on her back, spread-eagle. She was naked save for a lace bra and panty ensemble – a real trashy thing that Danny had ordered from one of his mother's lingerie magazines.

She was blindfolded with a rolled up bandana. Her wrists and ankles were bound to the bedposts with her own stockings. She didn't expect that Danny would tie them so tightly, that she would really be unable to move, or that she would find that fact both terrifying and arousing.

She could feel Danny's body heat pressing down. He was on his hands and knees on top of her.

'You look *sooo* fucking good,' he rasped with quivering, horndog anticipation. And then he leaned forward and began kissing her about the neck and shoulders. A euphoric pulse radiated out from each meeting of lips to naked skin, a mixture of fear and titillation. Danny moved down her torso, over the braided strap of her lace panties, to her inner thighs.

Abby had lied when she said she couldn't see. If she tilted her head back she could peek underneath the blindfold with her right eye. She did just that and watched Danny climb off of the bed and start to undress. He unbuttoned his shirt, let it slide from his shoulders.

Abby gasped, tugged against her restraints. Danny's skin was a chalky, ashen color accented with ugly blotches of deep red bordered in black. Just like he looked after lying dead in her apartment for a week.

There was a large wound in his chest where Abby had buried the kitchen knife. Dried blood marked the path it had traveled after leaking from his body. His eyes were clouded over, more dried blood caked around his nostrils.

'I thought you couldn't see me,' he said of her startled reaction. Then he unbuttoned and unzipped his pants. 'That's okay, though. Because I want you to see what I'm gonna do to you.' He let them fall to his ankles.

Abby screamed, but nothing came out. She tried to move, but was literally stuck to the bed.

There was a kitchen knife where Danny's cock should be; just like the one that Abby had buried in his chest. The handle melded with the fleshy stump of his cock like some mad scientist's idea of a joke. The damn thing was erect, pointing right at her, the blade stained with blood.

Abby tried again to scream and thrash, but accomplished neither. Her heart was pounding in her chest, threatening to explode as she watched Danny climb onto the bed and crawl up her body, the blade between his legs cutting a jagged path in the sheets.

'Don't worry babe,' he whispered. 'I'll be gentle.'

Abby awoke in a stupor, breathing like she had just run a marathon.

Just a dream, she smiled and took a deep, calming breath. She turned and was mildly startled to find Lori sitting at the other end of the bench looking like Hell. She stared straight ahead blankly, tears streaming from her eyes. One of them was nearly swollen shut.

'Oh God. Lori!' Abby cried out. 'I'm so sorry. I must've dozed off. Are you alright? How long have you been awake?'

'What happened?' Lori asked, through tears, her words slurred by a deep cut in her lip and the tender, swollen skin around it.

'You mean, you don't remember?'

Lori frowned, looking inward. The process appeared to cause her pain.

'I had gone upstairs to get away from Nanna and Gramps,' she remembered. 'I guess I must've fallen asleep. Then there was a loud noise from downstairs. It shook the whole cabin. I came down and… Oh God! Roxy was right,' she cried into her hands.

Abby wrapped a consoling arm around Lori's shoulders.

'He was standing over Gramps' wearing Geordi's clothes,' she said, sobbing as she spoke. 'Nanna was lying in the…'

Lori's head whipped toward the door of the cabin expecting to find her grandmother lying there. She met Nanna's absence with a confused look. The caved-in doorway appeared to jog a terrible memory.

'The sheriff and Roxy moved Nanna inside,' Abby informed her. Abby couldn't bring herself to help, so her job was to find some sheets from upstairs to cover the bodies. 'He didn't want you to—'

'Sheriff Taylor!' Lori remembered and looked around for the man. 'Where is he? Where's Roxy?'

'Hiking to the Stogies. John C. must have got to the radio in the sheriff's car. Slashed the tires, too. And he cut the phone line to the cabin. So there was no way for the sheriff to get outta here or to call for an ambulance. He's gonna use a phone at the Stogies.'

Lori seemed worried by that.

'They waited for you to wake up,' Abby told

her, 'but it was getting late. Sheriff Taylor wanted to get to the Stogie's before dark.'

Lori looked up at the sky. It was the ass end of daylight and the pre-dusk dim was starting to run its course.

'How long was I out?'

Abby hesitated. 'Two hours.'

'Two *freakin'* hours?'

'Me and Roxy wanted to carry you the whole way to the Stogies but the sheriff thought it best that we not move you until the paramedics get here. He said it shouldn't be more than a couple of hours, and they left around twenty minutes ago.'

Abby reckoned that her friend was experiencing some level of shock, so she made no effort to interrupt the awkward silence that followed.

'Nanna and Gramps...' Lori said finally, determined to take up her story again. 'They were already dead when I came downstairs. I screamed for him... for the cowboy to leave them alone. That's when he came after me. I tried to run for the door, but he was too fast. He tackled me and I must've hit my head because, the next thing I remember, I was coming to on the floor. I saw him change outta Geordi's clothes. My plan was to play dead, but then he grabbed the knife and came over to finish me off. I grabbed a sharp piece of wood waited until he got close. I stabbed him in his leg as hard as I could and ran out, but he caught me again on the porch and we fought and fought. He was so strong. I thought I was going to die.'

'But you didn't die, Lori,' Abby said triumphantly. 'You did what you had to do like I did with Danny. We're survivors, you and me.'

But Lori wasn't ready to play sisters just yet.

'I remember hearing the sheriff's voice,' she continued. 'Then gunshots. It felt like a weight had been lifted off me. The rest is blurry.'

'It'll come back to you whether you want it to or not,' Abby warned. 'Trust me—'

Lori looked out at the field and became suddenly preoccupied with a paisley-patterned bedsheet that lay crumpled in the grass several feet in front of the porch steps.

Abby looked too.

'What a minute,' she said, suddenly energized, her eyes darting to cover the entire field. 'Where's…'

'Where's what?' Lori asked, alarmed by Abby's mood swing.

'John C,' Abby said. 'His body was under that sheet.'

There was a noise from inside the cabin, where Nanna and Gramps' bodies were being kept. It sounded like deliberate movement.

THIRTY FOUR

'You wanna talk about it?' Roxy asked Sheriff Taylor as she hurried to catch up to him.

'Not really.'

Two words. Roxy mused. *Progress.*

The trail was so narrow that they had to walk single file. This made it easier for the sheriff to dismiss Roxy's attempts at conversation or to outright ignore them, which he had done several times since they started walking. When he did speak other than to remind Roxy to 'Hurry up,' it was via single word responses spat out the side of his head the way you'd address a nagging child.

They had just passed the intersecting trail that led to the boys' campsite and were wading out into the deep woods where the brush was much denser, and the phantom animal calls and insectoid clicks came thick and fast. The sky was but a jagged sliver between looming tree tops. Daylight was on its last legs.

Roxy muttered something about the incoming darkness which Sam, once again, just ignored. He was a few feet ahead of her, moving down the narrow dirt corridor cut deep into the Louisiana thicket with purpose. He handled the lumpy terrain and the curious tree limbs that reached out from either side like an expert.

Roxy, on the other hand, was having some trouble. She was choosing her footfalls carefully and using the trees for extra measure when needed. The terrain was unpredictable and she was wary of the sudden shifts in elevation and of the roots that tried to trip her up and of the branches that meant to fondle her.

'You've barely said a word since we started walking,' Roxy complained between heavy breaths. And when that didn't evoke a response, she added, 'Strong silent types have hearts, too. Don't they?'

Nanna and Gramps had this guy pegged all wrong. Based on their descriptions, Roxy had expected some sauced-up bumblefuck in the vein of Roscoe P. Coltrane. But Sheriff Taylor was much more complicated than that.

'Huh?' Sam frowned. His mind was elsewhere.

'I said, strong silent types have hearts, too. Don't they?'

Sam tossed a cockeyed look over his shoulder.

'Cause, you know how they say holding in your emotions in is bad for your heart?' Roxy said.

'I'll take my chances.'

Roxy looked up from the dirt to find the sheriff pulling away again and hurried to close the growing distance between them.

'Was that the first time you ever had to… you know—'

Sam stopped walking and turned to face Roxy. 'Look. I appreciate what you're trying to do, but I'm not gonna discuss the…' He searched for the right words and spoke them with a trace of humor. '*Psychological ramifications* of killing a man with—'

'—with what?' Roxy snapped back. 'With a stripper?'

'I was going to say with a kid.'

'Oh,' Roxy said, red-faced.

Sam eyes lingered on the girl for a moment, and then he turned, said 'C'mon,' and started walking.

Roxy fell into place a few strides behind him.

'You seem like a smart girl,' Sam said a few minutes later. 'How'd you wind up a stripper?'

'What? Strippers can't be smart?'

'Relax. It was just an observation. I've met my fair share in this line of work and let's just say they weren't the brightest bulbs in the box.'

'Well, maybe you need to expand your social circle,' Roxy shot back.

Between the tree tops, the jagged sliver of sky had settled into an evening tint. It brought a respite from the heat, but the light reaching down into the corridor was less scrutinizing as a result. There were dark spaces and ominous shapes where before there was only a crevice between converging trees or an orgy of low-level shrubs.

Roxy grew more tense with each deepening shade of blue. She quickened her pace, keen to stay within arm's reach of the sheriff.

'Lori's gonna be okay. Right?' she asked.

Sam pursed his lips. 'She took a few blows to the head…'

'Lori's tough. She'll pull through.'

'Yeah. I got that impression.'

'Are you gonna arrest her?'

Sam thought for a moment. 'I don't think anybody, in their right mind, would blame your friend for what she did back there. No man should be hittin' on a woman like that.'

Roxy found comfort in his answer. They kept walking.

'The answer is yes, by the way,' Sam offered.

Roxy was confused.

'You asked if that was the first time I killed a man. The answer is yes. And hopefully the last.'

***

'Lori!' Abby yelled for the fourth time with no response.

She was perched between the porch swing and the caved-in doorway of the cabin, afraid to venture any closer and risk catching a glimpse of all that death inside... again. As of today, Abby had seen enough death to last two lifetimes. Any more and her head might explode.

Lori had gone inside to investigate the noise they'd heard. She was literally off her ass and heading into the cabin before Abby could put two words together to stop her.

From inside, Abby heard Lori call out to Nanna as if trying to revive the dead matriarch. Then she heard someone gasp. And for the past five minutes, she had been standing there, before a darkening landscape, analyzing that very sound, and exploring possible causes.

Though she hadn't witnessed his actual death, Abby had seen John C.'s body lying in the grass. There was no way he was alive. No damn way. But then why wasn't Lori answering her? The cabin was no bigger than a shoebox. Lori had to have heard Abby calling for her.

Unless...

Abby made a move toward the caved-in doorway. She made another. And another. Soon she was standing at the outer edge of the broken doorframe. She called out to Lori one last time, and when her friend didn't answer, Abby took a deep breath and peered inside.

There were two bodies covered with paisley-patterned sheets. Nanna's sheet was pulled down to her chest, a painful grimace on her face. The old woman's eyes were wide open.

Abby recognized the legs sticking out of the other sheet as belonging to Gramps. The rest of the place looked fairly untouched.

The thud of hasty footsteps directed her eyes to the ceiling. Old wood shrieked and whined underfoot. Abby followed the footsteps to the top of the staircase where Lori appeared with a wooden baseball bat in her hand. Her eyes found Abby.

'Where the hell'd you get *that*?' Abby asked of the baseball bat.

'He's gone,' Lori said and then hurried down the steps. 'The cowboy's gone!'

'That's impossible,' Abby replied.

'Where is he then, Abby?! Huh?!'

Abby didn't have an answer. Her eyes darted around the room and found more cause for concern. She distinctly remembered seeing Geordi's clothing and his hollowed out, burlap head lying in a pile in the corner, where Lori said the cowboy had taken them off in haste. And now they were gone, too.

Lori took off toward the back door without warning. Following with her eyes, Abby realized that the back door was open.

'Lori!' Abby yelled in pursuit.

'If he's still alive, then he's gotta be injured, right?' Lori replied on the run.

"Injured" was an understatement. As such, Abby didn't know how to respond.

'Come on.' Lori turned and yelled before running out the door with the baseball bat firmly in hand. Her eyes were narrow and channeled aggression in a way that Abby had never seen before. 'We can get him before he gets away.'

It was all happening too fast for Abby to process in real time. Standing there, surrounded by death, her eyes moved around the room again as if she might find the cowboy's body stuffed in some corner that she, and Lori, had previously overlooked. But she found nothing, just old Voodoo knickknacks everywhere.

Abby thought of Lori's cleansing and of the eyes in the water – Christie Keller's eyes. If it was at all possible for someone in the cowboy's condition to get up and walk, than this house, these damn woods, was the place for it to happen.

Frustrated, Abby ran out onto the front porch, cupped her hands around her mouth, and yelled as loud as she could in the direction of the woods.

'Sheriff Taylor! Roxy! If you can hear me, come back!'

And then she waited.

It was darker than before, muted blue shades in the throes of deep-purple subjugation.

Even if they do hear you, they're far enough away that it'll take them a while to make it back, her inner voice chided. *In that time, Lori could be…*

Abby ran from the porch and sprinted over to the barn. She was calling out to Lori as she ran. The barn doors were open enough for Abby to squeeze through. Inside, the air was still and thick and stunk of hay.

Stepping cautiously, she moved forward and called out to her friend. She spotted a pair of legs sticking out from behind a stack of hay. They were a uniquely ambiguous shade, leaning way more toward light than dark. Abby knew that color well. The feet were wrapped in the shoes that she had purchased as a birthday gift for Lori.

Abby ran up to them.

'Oh my God! LORI!' She screamed.

Lori's body was in a seated position, squeezed between the stack of hay and the barn wall. Her eyes were closed. Her expression was oddly peaceful. Her head rested in a hard lean to one side. There was so much blood; more than Abby had ever seen. More than Danny's dying heart had pumped out through the knife-wound in his chest. It looked like someone had literally held the poor girl up by the feet and dipped her into a vat of the crimson liquid.

Lori had apparently been bludgeoned to death as evidenced by the bloody baseball bat lying across her lap and by the lack of noticeable hacking wounds.

Abby turned away, gagged. She stumbled towards the barn doors, shoved them open with both hands, and made for the woods. She ran until her lungs began to burn and there was no more breath to circulate through them. She needed to catch her breath lest she pass out and wind up dead as Lori and Nanna and Gramps.

Abby stopped and doubled over sucking wind. The severity of what she had just witnessed inside the barn settled in as her breath slowly returned.

Lori's dead. Your good friend, who you've

known since childhood. DEAD! Not just dead, but MURDERED in cold blood.

A strangely familiar melody haunted the air. It sounded like Gramps blowin' that same old bluesy riff on his harmonica. But that didn't make sense.

Abby peered over her shoulder, confused. Where was it coming from? The music seemed to be swirling around here somehow, coming from every direction she turned.

She saw the cabin in the distance, underneath a cloudless, purple sky with licks of yellow orange. Windows glared at her like eyes. The caved-in doorway was like a snarling mouth. The front door lay cockeyed inside the cracked frame, attached, by a single hinge, near the top. Abby remembered that door being open just moments ago.

The harmonica wailed. Abby felt compelled to run. Something bad was about to happen. It was almost like she was being warned. And then…

The haunting riff stopped as abruptly as it started. Beyond the tree-line, crickets and frogs sang acapella as the rest of the evening-shift woodland players warmed up for their performances.

One such sound – the whining of old wood – directed Abby to the front door of the cabin as it was slowly peeled open from the inside. She froze, adjusting her focus to see through the doorway, but it was too dark and she was too far away.

The woods became strangely quiet. The festering evening chill was on pause.

Seconds later, an aggressive shape thrust out of the darkness, cleared the porch steps in a single stride, and barrelled toward Abby like an angry bull. It was Geordi, the burlap man, his gloved fist wrapped tightly around the handle of the cane knife.

THIRTY FIVE

'You still there?' Roxy whispered at the massive oak tree standing before her.

'Where am I gonna go?' The tree responded in Sam Taylor's voice.

'Just checking.'

'Hurry. Would ja,' Sam harped. 'We still got a ways to go.'

'I'm hurryin'.'

They had been in the thick of it, fighting through the tangles when Roxy announced that she had to pee. She swore to an annoyed Sam that she had held it as long as possible.

The path had disappeared about a mile ago, swallowed up by the woods proper at the top of a steep ravine. Back then they were separated from the lake, and its tranquil flow, by fifty feet of angry, tangled shrubs, and the muddy, water-licked shoulder at the foot of the ravine.

Now she couldn't see more than a few feet through the blockade of oak stanchions and the minions of shrubs at hers and Sheriff Taylor's feet on either side. But she could still hear the faint sound of water licking the muddy shoreline below.

Standing from a squat, Roxy hiked up her panties and shorts in one pull and wiggled into them. She fastened her shorts and said, 'Okay.'

Sheriff Taylor walked out from behind the massive oak tree. He waved Roxy on, said 'Come on,' and started walking in the opposite direction.

Within seconds he was fighting with the natural lattice-work, pushing through with his bulk, swatting down branches, and bending them back enough to squeeze past.

Roxy looked down at her lacerated legs and wished for a hot tub to soothe the burning. A few random bruises and she would've been right at home at the Sugar Shack where all the biker chicks and the junkies, who'd fuck their own family members for a fix, danced. Watching the sheriff muscle through the tangles, Roxy took a deep breath and prepared for a long, hard fight. She soldiered forward following his path.

There was nothing left to say as they walked. Roxy had burned through her repertoire of small talk. She wondered how much longer until they reached the Stogies, but dared not ask. She'd have put them at an hour in, tops, but it could be more like half that. And at the rate they were moving, their ETA (as the sheriff put it) would be more like two-and-a-half, to three hours.

That's a long time to spend being spanked and groped by nature. Two-and-a-half-to-three hours was a hell of a long time to spend with her imagination and the all-consuming darkness of the woods.

The air was filled with voices speaking in nature's many languages. *All talking about us, no doubt,* Roxy mused.

Roxy tripped over an exposed root and grabbed hold of the sheriff's shirt to keep from falling. The sudden movement startled Sam, who tossed an annoyed glare over his shoulder. He had been doing that a lot.

They pressed forward through the molesting foliage. Five minutes seemed to pass in fifteen with little progress.

'Wait!' yelled an excited Roxy. 'Didju hear that?'

She could've sworn she heard her name being called.

'I heard *YOU*,' the sheriff said as if on his last nerve.

'No. Listen.'

This time Sam wasn't having it. He stopped, turned to face her. 'No, *you* listen,' he said. 'I get it! Okay, I get that you're not from around here – that the woods ain't your thing. I get that you're afraid we won't make it back to the cabin in time to save your friend. I get that you're tired and that your legs are so cut up that you might as well be dancing at the Tailgate. I get all that. But you're not making things any easier by constantly reminding—'

This time they both heard the voice. It was faint, but there was no mistaking that it had called out Roxy's name.

'Abby!' Roxy cried out and ran toward the source of the voice.

Sam followed.

The brush had recovered quickly from their

initial trek through. Sam's improvised trail was nearly gone. Holding her arms in front of her face as she bullrushed forward, Roxy leapt and ducked without a moment's hesitation. The terror in Abby's voice drove her on.

'Rox-xeeee!'

Abby's voice was louder this time, her desperation and terror more relatable from the closer distance.

'We're comin', Abby!' Roxy yelled back with equal emotion.

'Stay calm,' the sheriff reprimanded between huffs.

The girls found each other just outside the tangles, where the trail had gone rogue. Abby didn't look like herself. Her face was beet red. Her hair was weighted down by sweat and stuck to her face. Her shirt was equally soaked and clinging to her small frame in a way that accentuated her petite, hourglass figure. She had the look of death in her eyes.

'Roxy,' Abby cried.

She ran up and collapsed in her friend's arms as if she had spent every last drop of energy reaching her and had no more left. She was breathing heavily, like she might never recover from exhaustion.

'What is it? Where's Lori?'

But Abby could only return gibberish between desperate gasps for air.

'Your friend,' Sam leaned in and said, 'where is she?'

'She's dead! He killed her!' Abby managed.

The sheriff looked up, suddenly energized.

Roxy let go of Abby and backed away, her

eyes full of disbelief and knowing.

'*WHO* killed her?!' Sam demanded to know.

'It was Geordi… the cowboy.'

'That's impossible!'

'He's alive!' Abby said.

'No,' Roxy argued. 'You shot him in the head,' she said to Sam. 'And then, Lori got 'em with the knife…' She paused. 'He can't be alive.'

'He's alive! And he's out there!' Abby motioned as if to run away. 'We have to go.'

Sam grabbed hold of Abby's arm.

'Wait-a-second.' He pulled her into his grasp, placed his hands firmly on her shoulders, and looked her in the eyes. 'Now calm down and tell me what happened.'

Abby took several breaths, and then said, 'We were waiting on the porch when we heard a noise from inside the cabin. Lori ran inside to see what it was. I went in after her and we saw that the cowboy's body was gone. Lori ran out to the barn to look for him.' She hesitated. 'That's where I found her.'

Abby became emotional.

'Seeing Lori like that… There was so much blood…'

'Then what?' Sam said. 'What makes you think it was the cowboy?'

'BECAUSE HE CAME AFTER ME!' Abby shouted. 'He chased me into the woods. I ran and ran until I saw you guys.'

Something moved further down the path that Abby had just travelled. Sam snatched his gun from the holster.

Gramps' song played again, haunting the

night with its melancholy echo. Their eyes shot up to the tops of the trees as if they expected to find the owner of the song perched on a branch.

Roxy felt a shiver run down her spine. Gramps was dead. There was no way in hell someone could survive what John C. had done to him. And there was no way in hell John C. could've survived what the sheriff and then Lori had done to *him*. Did that make Abby a liar? Had she snapped and killed Lori, herself?

'Tha fuck is that?' Sam said of the wailing harmonica riff.

'I don't know how to explain it,' Abby said, 'but I think it's some sort of warning.'

Something moved again. It sounded like sticks breaking underfoot. The sound had come from behind a large tree standing at a crooked lean in the same general vicinity as the previous sound.

Sam lifted his gun and motioned for the girls to stay back. He stepped cautiously toward the tree up ahead.

'Come out with your hands up, whoever you are!' He stated in his most authoritative voice.

The harmonica wailed.

'Come out with your hands up, I said! Or else I'm gonna come in there after you!'

The girls stood close together.

Sam crept up to the tree. When he was a few feet from it, he thrust himself forward and jumped into a wide-legged, two-handed shooting pose. But there was only empty space behind the tree.

Sam exhaled. He dropped his arms, looked over at the girls, and shook his head.

There was a terrible odor like something twice dead. Just then a hooded figure exploded from the shrubs and tackled the sheriff into the brush on the other side of the path. They tumbled down the embankment in a violent embrace.

Momentum eventually pulled them apart and they fell the rest of the way separately.

Sam face-planted on the muddy shoreline. He thrust himself to his hands and knees and rubbed the mud from his eyes. He felt a burning sensation around his abdomen, looked down to find a line of singed fabric along the front of his shirt where his attacker's arm had made contact. He searched the ground for his gun. His heart sank when it was evident that he wouldn't find it any time soon, and then he sprung to his feet ready to defend despite being rightly dazed.

Sam saw his attacker coming to a stand ten feet away. It was Geordi, the burlap man. Sam's gut told him to hold his dismay, as it could've been anyone beneath the mask. That, however, wouldn't explain the living rot that engulfed Geordi's entire form. Crackling like ethereal flames, the Devil Vapor infected everything within a foot and a half of the burlap man with its withering, wilting spell. Debris rose like embers and evaporated in the supernatural heat. The weird words and symbols on Geordi's face appeared to be moving, too.

The tumble down the ravine had disarmed Geordi. His cane knife was impaled in the mud a few feet away. Geordi pointed his face at the knife and then turned to Sam and tilted his head as if to say, 'I dare you!'

Sam thought he saw those exact words emerge from the swarming red scribble on Geordi's burlap face .

Sam went for the knife and woke up seconds later, on his back. There was a sharp pain across the front of his face.

The burlap man had retrieved the cane knife and was walking toward him. There was no time to stand so Sam crawled backward. Through Geordi's legs he saw another man in the background and thought, at first, that he was hallucinating.

The other man wore denim cut-offs that were way too short and a white tee with a Levi's logo across the chest. And goddammit if he wasn't a spittin'-image of Tom Skerrit, the actor. The other man had apparently been startled by their sudden entrance; almost like he was caught in the act, kneeling in front of a hollowed out tree stump stuffed with what looked like doll parts, clothing, tools, and a film projector spliced to a car battery.

In the time it took for Sam to clock the other man, Geordi had closed the distance between them.

Sam turned away from the sudden rush of heat and hid his face behind his arm. He felt his skin began to blister as the Devil Vapor singed his clothing and hair, and cooked his flesh. He peeked through the deadly mist and saw Geordi lift the big knife over his head. This time there was no mistaking the words that materialized from the swarming red scribble on his burlap dome. They came one-at-a-time, manifesting in an emphatic, black font.

DIE!
PIG!
DIE!

Sam yelled as loud as he could for the girls to 'RUN!' and prepared to meet his maker. At the very least he'd go out like a hero. Maybe the honour of dying in the line of duty would prevail over all the marital indiscretions Whitney would have dragged out in court. Maybe Whitney would be so distraught that she would hold her tongue, not mention that one time he'd lost his temper with her. Sam braced himself for the final blow.

A ping pong-sized rock hit Geordi in the back of his doomed head. A male voice came on its heels. 'Stop!'

The burlap man's arm froze in mid-swing. He whipped his head toward the voice and found Jeff Sedaris, on one knee, broadcasting instant regret. Geordi lowered his arm, spun around, and started walking toward the man.

Jeff Sedaris stood up and threw his hands out in front of him.

'Hey. Look. No hard feelings,' Jeff said, attempting a smile while simultaneously working to digest the approaching menace.

The featureless, burlap dome came alive with a swarm of red scribble.

That damn mist in its trail laid waste to everything it touched. Fragments of withered death wafted upward and evaporated in the swampy heat. It was like one of those crazy sci-fi movies Jeff would work on only with better special effects.

'Jeeeesus! Mary! And Joseph!' Jeff cried out, watching it all happen and clocking the very large knife in the burlap man's hand.

Jeff backed away and tripped over the old film projector on the ground.

The projector switch toggled 'On' and cast a ray of light onto the burlap man's torso.

A miniature ballerina danced in slow motion within the rectangle of light cast on the front of Geordi's old P-coat. A few seconds later and the same girl was just standing there, staring blankly forward. And then she was dancing again.

The weird performance ran over and over on a few seconds' loop.

The footage was grainy, but deliberately so. The girl was young, no more than twelve years old, with pale skin. She wore a knee-length night gown with lace borders that flowed like an apparition. She was clearly meant to look like Christie Keller.

The burlap man stopped and looked down at the image. He watched briefly before looking up. His head tilted to one side as he waved a scolding finger at Jeff Sedaris.

Jeff turned to run and collided with an eavesdropping oak tree, falling flat on his back. A dark clothed leg appeared on either side of his face. His eyes burned. The skin on his face began to blister and melt.

Jeff flailed at the burning, stinging sensation and attempted to wriggle away. He cried out 'No! No! No!' in rapid succession and then

screamed like a girl as Geordi hacked at his torso and head until there was no sign of life left
save for the involuntary twitching of nerves.

Afterward, the burlap man turned to locate
his other prey. But the sheriff and the two girls
were long gone.

THIRTY SIX

The two girls ran, following the ethereal harmonica that seemed to be calling them.

Roxy led the charge, Abby trailing by little
more than a pace. Both girls were cut head to
toe, ugly welts rising up from where Mother
Nature had had her way with them.

They reached a clearing with a grand looking RV, parked in the middle.

Inside the RV, a woman with tanned skin
and raven hair paced from window-to-window
speaking angrily into a walkie talkie.

Roxy grabbed Abby by the arm and made
for the RV.

Roxy opened the RV door and clambered inside, Abby behind her.

'Come in, Goddammit!' Elaine Sedaris
yelled into her receiver. 'All that belly-achin'
about ME not screwing things up... And you
pull a stunt like this?!'

The door to the RV suddenly burst open.
Elaine turned sharply, prepared to give Jeff a
piece of her mind but instead was met by two
girls.

'Hey, you can't come in here!' Elaine hollered at them.

'We just need to use your radio!' the blonde
one gasped.

Elaine suddenly recognized the other one
from somewhere, the mousy one.

'Hey, aren't you..?'

But the kid was quickly distracted, eyeing
up the Newspaper clippings on the walls and
the wigs resting atop mannequin heads on the
countertop and all the recording equipment
and cameras lying around. A handful of Polaroids were spread out on the kitchenette table
and she lifted some and flicked through them.

'I said, you can't be in here,' Elaine said
again.

'Hey! What's the matter with you?!' the
blonde girl protested. 'We just need to use your
radio. We have to call the cops! Peoples' lives
are in danger!'

Call the cops? Elaine stepped back, her eyes
speaking for her. She looked on the girls with
suspicion, trying to gauge their intentions. She
focused on the one she recognized.

'Wait-a-minute,' she said, pointing. 'I remember you from the other day at the lake.
What's this, some kinda sting operation?'

The mousy girl didn't respond. She was still
obsessing over the Polaroids.

'You stay away from those!' Elaine growled.

The blonde girl used the distraction to move
on the walkie-talkie, snatching it up in one
quick thrust, and running for the door. Elaine
grabbed hold of her shirt and tried to pull her
back, but was instead pulled off-balance herself.

They came stumbling out of the RV together. Elaine was on the blonde girl's back reaching around her body for the radio. The blonde girl was just as determined to keep it from her. She curled inward and blocked Elaine's multi-armed attacks with her shoulders and hips. They were grunting and cursing each other.

Inside the RV, Abby scanned the Polaroids thoroughly. She noticed that the subjects all appeared unaware that they had been photographed. Except for a few of them, the subject's name was scrawled at the bottom of each photo in red or black marker. Abby saw several people she didn't recognize, horribly ordinary folks with names like 'Bob', and 'Hank', and 'Tessa', and 'Barbra-Jean.'

Many of the photos were taken here at the Stogies. She found a photo of Roxy, then one of Lori. She found one of herself, taken on the first night during Lori's 'cleansing.' It was an awful photo. Her eyes were closed. Her head was slumped forward. She looked like a druggie.

She looked some more and found John C. and his friends. Nanna and Gramps were there, too.

Abby's eyes scrolled left, drawn to a doll sprawled on the bed in the back of the RV. Based on the clothing and hair, she assumed that the doll was supposed to be Christie Keller.

Lying on the floor beside the bed was a clutter of fake doll heads on sticks. The sticks were approximately a foot in length and stained with dirt, and caked mud from the tip, up to the bottoms of the eyes. There was scuba gear lying nearby; the same scuba gear that the woman – Elaine Sedaris was her name, Abby recalled – had been wearing when they first met.

Abby revisited the memory of eyes in the lake. She imagined Elaine beneath the surface in her scuba gear operating the various heads, and succumbed to a rush of embarrassment.

The two young women were going at it outside the camper. Some of the other residents had come out of their tents, and cabins, and campers to see what was going on. A small crowd formed in the main area, where the Sedaris' RV was parked.

'You alright?' an older gentlemen who could've been Santa's skinny twin asked Elaine Sedaris.

'I caught this girl and her friend trying to break into my trailer,' Elaine appealed to the man. 'The other one's still inside.'

A male resident crept up to the RV and stood on his toes to look in the window.

'No! That's not true,' the blonde girl argued as Skinny Santa and another man walked up and pulled her off of Elaine. 'We just wanted to use her walkie-talkie to radio the cops!'

The man by the camper said, 'Yeah. There's another girl inside.' He took a few steps back, cupped his hands over his mouth and yelled at the window, 'Come on out here now, missy!'

'You leave her alone!'

'Now calm down young lady,' Skinny Santa said to the blonde girl. 'What you want the PO-lice for?'

The RV door opened and the mousy girl – *Abby, that was her name*, Elaine recalled –

stepped out looking like she had seen a hundred ghosts. She looked at the gathered crowd, said, 'There's a killer out there. He killed our friends. He killed Sheriff Taylor…'

'Sheriff Taylor?' someone said as if the name meant something to them.

'…and if you don't let us call the cops, he's probably going to kill all of you, too.'

Some of the crowd reacted fearfully, but most were suspicious of her story.

Elaine capitalized on their skepticism and said, 'See what I mean?'

'You sure you and your friend ain't on somepthin,' Skinny Santa accused.

'She's telling the truth,' her friend said.

'You'd all know it if this *BITCH* wasn't so reluctant to let us call the cops,' Abby said, shooting daggers at Elaine Sedaris. 'I know what you're up to; you and your husband.

'I don't know what you're talking about,' a nervous Elaine interrupted.

'They've been faking Christie Keller sightings,' Abby said to the crowd.

'What?! That's ridiculous'

Abby pointed inside the cabin. 'She's got pictures of all of you in there. Look for yourself!'

'What's she talkin' about, Lanie,' some woman asked.

Skinny Santa let go of the blonde girl, said, 'Enough-a-this.' He walked over and snapped the walkie-talkie from Elaine. The man gave her a look that was not at all Santa-like. 'I'm gonna get to the bottom of this myself,' he said.

The blonde girl tossed a victorious sneer at

Elaine, who turned and stomped off toward her camper. Abby moved out of Elaine's way as she pushed past her, climbed up into the RV and slammed the door behind her.

A burst of static and a distorted voice came from the walkie-talkie.

Skinny Santa's opened his mouth to respond.

There was a whoosh sound from the brush just beyond Elaine's camper. A silver blur cut through the air and lodged itself deep into Skinny Santa's chest. The force spun him like a drunken ballerina. The radio flew from his limp grasp. His body smacked the dirt and lay there motionless.

Screams followed. Frightened residents scattered.

Roxy was on her ass, where she'd landed when the other man, who was holding her, panicked and shoved her aside before he ran away. She looked up to see the burlap man emerge from the darkness as if launched from a canon. He approached her like a man on a mission, snatching the cane knife from the fallen corpse without looking.

He was on top of Roxy before she knew it, standing cock-sure and tapping the blade against the palm of his gloved hand. She could feel the heat from the Devil Vapor. The terrible odor made her eyes water.

A primal growl from behind. 'NO MORE!'

Abby jumped on the burlap man's back intent on beating him about the head and shoulders with a closed fist, but instead screamed at the sudden rush of pain and immediately pushed herself off of him. She fell down, slapped her hands over her eyes, and rubbed them feverishly. Her forearms and the backs of her hands bubbled up in blisters like she'd held them under boiling water.

Roxy crawled over to Abby while the burlap man straightened his clothing and his mask and then cricked his neck from side-to-side. She slid her feet underneath her, and attempted to drag Abby to safety, but Geordi stepped in her way. He was tapping the blade against his palm again.

The swarming red scribble spat out a string of words.

**THIS
IS
GONNA
HURT**

Roxy cast a defiant glare up at the burlap man, yelled, 'FUCK! YOU!'

Geordi raised the knife over his head. A single word morphed from the swarm.

BITCH!

An engine revved. The burlap man was suddenly illuminated. Geordi whipped toward the light and met the grill of a speeding pickup truck with a thud that echoed into the night. His limp body went flying thirty feet into the deep Louisiana brush.

Brake pads squealed. Big wheels locked, kicking up dirt.

The pickup slid to a stop at the edge of the brush. The grill was damaged from the collision with Geordi's torso. The headlights cast a harsh glow into the deep.

Sheriff Sam Taylor stared groggily through the windshield of the pickup as if waiting for Geordi to climb to his feet so that he could hit him with the truck again. His head begin to sway. His eyes rolled back. His head slumped forward onto the steering wheel. The horn blared.

Roxy ran up to the driver's side window of the pickup and lifted Sam's head off of the steering wheel.

'Oh my God! Sheriff! Are you alright?!'

'Hey! That's my truck!' someone yelled.

Roxy opened the door of the pickup and moved in closer to Sheriff Taylor. She slapped his face, trying to revive him. Abby came up behind her. She was holding her forearms against her body. Her eyes were red and swollen and leaking tears.

'He's hurt bad,' Roxy said to her just as the sheriff's eyes fluttered, and then opened slightly.

'Did we get him?' he asked, half-conscious.

'Yeah. I think you did,' Roxy replied.

Abby watched the group of mostly male residents who had armed themselves with shotguns and were walking out into the illuminated area ahead of the pickup, looking for the burlap man's corpse.

One of them eventually yelled back, 'He ain't here!'

THIRTY SEVEN

'I can't speak about the case,' said Dr Fred Bonaparte as he walked across the parking lot toward the throng of well-dressed people blocking the entrance to the Black Water Medical Examiner's office. 'So, please don't waste your breath.'

Microphones were thrust at the silver-haired gentleman. Several voices spoke at once, ambushing him with questions they weren't meant to ask.

The crowd parted and Dr Bonaparte pushed his way past. The reporters yipped and barked until he disappeared behind glass double doors. Afterward, they crowded the doors and watched. Some continued shouting questions into the glass.

'It's been like that all morning,' a nervous security guard informed the doctor when he entered the lobby.

The Black Water Medical Examiner's Office was also the headquarters of the town's General Practitioner For thirty years it was a one-man operation run by Dr Bonaparte. These days he only came in on special occasions. The 'Black Water Voodoo Murders,' as the media had named it, was one such occasion.

Sheriff Taylor had asked that the doctor personally oversee the handling of the bodies in the basement while he figured things out. He didn't trust that the doctor's staff could resist the media's seductive pull and it was his intention to keep the details quiet lest the state boys and the Feds came knocking sooner rather than later.

In the three days since the news vans and the hungry reporters arrived, they had tried several times to extort information from staff and patients as they came and went. Some of them had gone as far as posing as patients and delivery men in an attempt to gain access to the morgue.

'There're supposed to be two guards on duty,' Bonaparte said to the man, clearly annoyed by the second guard's absence.

The first guard looked sheepish.

'He's upstairs, sir.'

Bonaparte looked around the small lobby and frowned. The receptionist wasn't at her desk. The nurse's station next to the reception desk was empty. The door leading to the examination rooms had been left open and the doctor could see that there was no one back there. Personal effects had been left in waiting room chairs. Screamin' Jay Hawkins was putting a spell on them from the waiting room speakers.

'Everyone's upstairs,' the guard added. 'They've been waiting outside your office, since...'

'Since what?' the doctor snapped.

The guard hesitated.

'Best you see for yourself.'

The staircase door flew open and coughed up a young nurse looking all kinds of flustered. A small rectangle of brass was pinned above her left breast, "Nurse Hawkins" engraved on the face.

'Oh, there you are,' she said to the doctor.

'Could somebody explain to me what the Sam Hill is going on around here?' Bonaparte snarled. 'I leave you people alone for one morning and you all lose your damn minds?!'

'It's not what you think, doctor,' Nurse Hawkins replied.

'And what, pray tell—' the doctor started to say.

'You really should hear her out, sir,' the guard interrupted.

Bonaparte looked the man over, almost like he was offended. Afterward, he turned back to the nurse, said, 'Now, I know my hearin' isn't what it used to be, but I'll be damned if I didn't get a phone call from you about half-an-hour ago regarding one of the victims – a woman who's been on ice for just under a week, I might add – who just miraculously woke up and started having conversations with people. Do you realize how that sounds?

Nurse Hawkins started to respond, but the doctor cut her off.

'Do you have any idea how it would make us look if those vultures out there were to hear any of this nonsense?'

'Nurse Guthrie saw her first,' the woman persisted.

'Where is she?'

'She's lying down in the back. She's too traumatized to talk right now.'

'Traumatized,' Bonaparte said, unconvinced. 'What the hell was Nurse Guthrie doing there in the first place?'

'She admits that she shouldn't have been in there,' Nurse Hawkins confessed. 'She said she

225

was curious, what with all the attention over the murders and everything…'

The doctor shook his head, made a face.

'It was the old Sawyer woman. She was just sittin' there on the edge of the table when Nurse Guthrie came in and turned on the lights. We heard her scream from upstairs in the lobby. We ran down and saw her passed out on the floor outside the morgue. We were trying to revive her when someone started knocking on the morgue door, from the other side. We thought maybe somebody had got locked in, but when we opened it, she was standing there… the Sawyer woman… Dead as can be… but… alive. "Tell the sheriff. It's not John C. It's not the cowboy," she kept saying in this weird voice. We told her that we couldn't make that call. Then she kept asking who was in charge. So, we called you.'

Bonaparte glanced over at the guard as if waiting to be let in on the joke.

'Did you witness this, too?'

'No, sir,' the guard replied. 'But Nurse Guthrie ain't one to lie, that's all I know.'

'She's waiting for you in your office,' the nurse said. 'The Sawyer woman.'

There were six people crowding the short hallway that stretched from the stairwell and single elevator to Dr Bonaparte's office. They stood, and leaned, and sat together on the floor awaiting the doctor's arrival on pins and needles. The small group perked up when Dr Bonaparte exited the stairwell. Nurse Hawkins walked in after him and directed his attention to his office door.

'In there.'

'I know where my office is. Thank you.'

The people sitting on the floor stood up. One of those people was Dr Vetner, Bonaparte's second in command.

'Dr Bonaparte. You're here,' the younger doctor said. He appeared nervous, unprepared. His hands were shaking. He looked on the older doctor with eyes that had seen too much.

Looking around the small space, Dr Bonaparte picked up on similar characteristics in the other members of the small group.

'You allowed the patients to see all this?' Bonaparte scolded while casting a roving glare at the three non-staff members of the group.

'Well. Ahhh… it all happened so fast,' Dr Vetner replied.

'And it ain't everyday that you see something like that,' the other security guard walked up and added.

Dr Bonaparte pushed past the men and walked to his office door under the watchful eyes of the group. He grabbed the doorknob, turned, and looked back as if to give the others one more chance to let him in on the joke. But they simply stared in terrified anticipation.

He turned the knob and pushed the door open.

There was a naked, black woman seated in the chair front of his desk with her back to the door. She was dark-skinned, but with a chalky, ashen layer. Her beefy arms rested on several folds of skin that peeked out from the sides of the high seatback. Her head was strangely deflated. Aside from that, she looked like any other patient awaiting the doctor's prognosis.

The undead Sawyer woman turned stiffly and looked at the stunned doctor. Every movement was scored by the crackle-crunch of dead muscle and flesh, and brittle old bones. There was a strange glow in her completely white eyes, something resembling life, but not alive. It contradicted the rest of her face, which hung slack. Her rounded shoulders, too. Her lips were dry and cracked. Her hair was a disheveled headdress of graying, black wisps. A Y-shaped autopsy incision had been sutured closed across her upper chest. The incision was clean and neat, with no flaying of skin. The suture-pattern indicated an experienced hand. These were Dr Bonaparte's trademarks.

'Are you in charge?!' Undead Nanna said to the doctor in a strange, hollow voice.

THIRTY EIGHT

Sheriff Sam Taylor sat in his car, parked outside the court house.

He'd left the radio on, listening to the few calls that bounced back and forth between Edna and whoever was out there on patrol. There was some domestic dispute going on and it weighed heavy on Sam's heart given the music he was likely to face himself in ten or so minutes whenever he mustered the courage to get his ass on into that all-too familiar building he was parked in front of.

He shifted in his seat, winced at the sudden jab of pain that ran up his side. That whole trouble up at the Sawyers' place a week ago had left him with a few broken ribs and his arm in a sling. Damn near made it impossible dressing himself this morning and he hadn't been able to iron his shirt the way he'd have liked. He could have asked Edna, of course, but Sam just hadn't felt too moved to do that or do much of anything else of late. Truth of the matter was, the fact he'd even managed to show up today at all, never mind put a suit on for the occasion, surprised him.

Sam reached inside his glove compartment, pushed aside the service revolver holstered in there, and found what he was looking for.

Dutch courage, that's what's got me through, he mused, flipping the canteen to his mouth and taking a healthy swig.

He peered at the courthouse doors, watching as some suited and booted lawyer type pushed through.

He'd be surprised if that Symons woman from the local rag wasn't in there yet, perched in the public gallery, notepad and pen at the ready. And he knew there'd be plenty for her to scribble about once Whitney's lawyer had had his little dance. The cat was going to be truly let out of the bag, make no mistake about that.

The radio hissed pulling Sam out of his maudlin thoughts.

'Sam, you out there?'

He sighed, went to turn off the dial.

'Don't you hang up on me, Sheriff.'

Sam blew some air out and then picked up the receiver.

'Edna, I'm kinda busy right now. Can't this wait?'

'No, I don't think it can,' she said. 'Got Dr Bonaparte here with me and he says it's important.'

Bonaparte? Sam mused. *What could he want?*

'Give me that damn thing,' another voice said before Edna was gone and a male voice replaced her. 'Sam, it's Fred Bonapart here and…' he breathed a heavy sigh before continuing, 'Well, we had ourselves a miracle of modern science down at the lab today. I don't know how to say this, or how it happened, but it seems we, er, got it wrong with that old Sawyer woman you had delivered to us.'

'Got it wrong? What do you mean, got it wrong?' Sam pressed.

'What I mean is that she, and I still don't know how to explain it but I saw it with my own eyes…'

'Get to the point, Fred.'

'Well, she wasn't just as… dead as we thought she were, is all.'

Sam laughed involuntarily. 'What the hell are you talking about, man?'

'What I'm talking about, Sam, is coming into my office to find a dead woman talking to me,' Bonaparte said, his voice suddenly raised. 'And don't tell me that ain't possible cos I already know it but that's how it was and she had a message she needed me to pass onto you before she could lie back down on that slab and be dead again.'

Sam swallowed hard. He could feel the receiver slipping in the palm of his suddenly moist hand and gripped it tightly. He thought of all the crazy, unexplained stuff that had gone down up at that cabin. The burlap man with that crazy writing dancing around his cloth-covered dome, that damn vapor that swirled round about him, killing every root and branch it touched, all those bodies going missing without a trace, including the Sawyer girl who they were meant to have found in the barn and, well, did not find. And here was the thing: deep down Sheriff Sam Taylor, a skeptical man by nature, knew the natural world alone couldn't explain what had happened up there in those woods and, God knew, he was suddenly open to a little of the supernatural.

'What did she say?' Sam asked Bonaparte in a small voice. 'Just tell me what she said.'

THIRTY NINE

Roxy couldn't hear too well in the club but the words, 'It wasn't Lane. It wasn't the cowboy,' was all she needed.

She slammed the phone down and made for the door.

'Hey, babe, where you going?' some no-mark protested, making a grab for her, but she steered around him, pushed through the doors out onto the sidewalk.

She must have looked a sight, dressed like a hooker in plain daylight. This was still the South, no matter whether you were in the city or not, and folks still had certain standards that a working Roxy flaunted daily. She caught a glimpse of herself as she clattered along the street, all heels and lipstick, the leather skirt barely covering her ass. But she'd no time to change if what Sheriff Taylor was saying meant what she thought it meant.

The killer was still out there.

And her girl Abby was on her own right now, thinking herself lucky after a few close shaves.

Roxy stepped off the sidewalk, hailing a cab, but none were for stopping, figuring her to be a whore.

'Hey!' she called at one, hooking her finger after the driver slowed, looked her up and down, then sped up again.

Finally, one pulled over. Roxy jumped in, gave Abby's address and they were away.

The driver was Indian. He wore a Turban and had some charms and shit hanging from his mirror. Roxy caught him checking out her reflection. He smiled at her, winked. Roxy crossed her legs and tried her damnedest to pull the skirt further down her thighs. It wasn't for moving.

They turned a corner into 4th Street, the distracted driver all but slamming into the back of a tail of traffic. Roxy was almost thrown out of her seat.

'What is it? What's happening?' she asked.

'Traffic,' he said, illustrating the obvious by pointing at the cars in front.

'Yes, I can see that,' Roxy snapped, 'but why?'

The driver shrugged. Didn't matter to him. His eyes fell on the meter, still ticking away.

Roxy slumped back into her seat.

'Come on,' she whispered.

She thought of the cowboy, of how sure she'd been he was the killer from the very start. How she and the sheriff had found him at the cabin struggling with Lori, poised to kill her.

Jesus, who the hell else could it have been?

But Roxy trusted Sheriff Taylor. He was measured, didn't seem to be a man who made rash decisions. If he said the killer was still out there, that they'd got the wrong man, Roxy was going to believe him.

The cab driver messed with the dial on his stereo, trying to find a station he liked. He turned the dial back and forth, shaking his head at the flaky reception he was getting.

Wailing harmonica suddenly started playing, a station not quite catching.

Roxy startled at its sound. 'Wait,' she said. 'What is that?'

But the cabbie ignored her, settling on some talk show or other and leaving it at that.

She reached for the grigri bag dangling from her neck, pinched it between her fingers and thumb at the memory of Gramps. While in the hospital she had dreamed of the old man watching her sleep, sitting back in that chair of his, shotgun laid across his lap.

Later, she found the grigri bag in a sack with the rest of her clothing from that night and, slipping it around her neck, was overcome by a strong feeling of protection.

She didn't question how it got with her stuff.

The traffic was starting to move. There were two cars pulled over at the side of the road, one crumpled at the front and the other banged in at the back. A cop was waving cars past but everyone was craning for a look at what happened.

Roxy looked at the meter. It was over ten dollars and she had forgotten to bring her handbag. She didn't care. Once they got to Abby's place, she was out of the cab and running. Unpaid fares were the least of her worries.

They reached the apartment block. Roxy hardly waited for the car to stop before she reached for the door. It was locked.

She looked to the cabbie but his hands remained on the wheel, his eyes watching her in the mirror.

'You pay,' he said.

'Look,' she said, smiling nervously, 'I haven't got any cash on me. But my friend does. I'll come back down and pay you once I see her.'

But the cabbie wasn't having any of it. 'You pay,' he insisted.

From somewhere in the building, Roxy heard a scream. She craned her neck to look up and saw the light on in Abby's apartment. Had to have come from there.

'Please,' she said, 'My friend's in trouble, she—'

'You pay now!' cried the cabbie. His hand was outstretched, palm facing upwards. His face was hard and furrowed like dried clay.

Roxy spotted his farebook and pen. She grabbed it, started to scribble something. 'It's my address and phone number,' she said, ripping the page out and offering it. 'I'll pay up, promise I will. Please, you have to let me out.'

He shook his head, threw the page to one side. His eyes suddenly widened, like he'd thought of something else. He pointed one tanned finger at Roxy's chest, made a kind of beckoning gesture.

'What?'

'Show me,' he said, still pointing at her chest.

It dawned on Roxy what he meant. 'You must be fucking kidding?'

Another scream from the apartment.

The cabbie wagged his finger again.

'Okay, okay,' Roxy said. She pulled her boob tube down, pulled out one tit.

The cabbie reached beneath his robes, starting rubbing himself.

'Again!' he yelled and she realized he wanted to see the other breast, so she hooked the boob tube right down, both breasts hanging out. She wished to hell she'd worn a bra tonight but it hardly seemed to matter, working at a strip joint.

Precious moments passed as the cabbie continued to work himself.

'Come on!' Roxy yelled.

He was panting, all out of breath, sweat building on his forehead.

'Oh for Christ's sake,' Roxy screamed, reaching her hand into the front and grabbing his cock. It was short and stumpy and she put a lot of wrath into yanking it. This seemed to excite him, his face twisting and reddening, his breath shortening until his pelvis started to shake and the glory days were coming. The bells hanging from his mirror started to ring.

Roxy fell back, wiped her hand on the seat. 'Now open the fuck up!' she screamed.

The cabbie clicked the doors and Roxy was out running. She tripped on a broken heel, stumbled before unfastening both shoes and continuing in her bare feet.

FORTY

Whitney was talking, yabbering on about all the things he'd never done, about what a bad husband he was, but Sam Taylor didn't care. He wasn't listening. His mind was elsewhere, going over the news he'd just received from the morgue, the news that didn't make any sense, yet made a lot of sense in a place with a rep like Black Water. But mostly, he thought about those girls he'd been called to protect and the piss poor job he'd done at that.

Roxy could be in danger.

Sam stood suddenly to his feet.

His lawyer, a slick-haired cretin called Mc-Bain stared at him, eyes creased in a 'What the fuck are you doing?' kind of way.

'I'm sorry,' Sam whispered. He looked to the judge, apologized more audibly, then filed out of the benches.

He made for the door.

Everyone started to talk at once. The judge was banging his hammer, telling him to sit down, but Taylor ignored him.

A court official approached but Sam gave him a look that made him back away and left the court room.

He retrieved his badge and gun from security. Spotted a payphone on his way out, thought of calling Roxy again but then figured she'd be on her way over to Abby's place. He knew Abby's address but didn't have her number.

He reached his car, went to open the door.

A hand pressed on his shoulder and he swung around nervously, finding Whitney.

She wiped tears from her face, said, 'Sam, I won't let you do this. For Christ's sake, this is important to me!'

'Not now, Whitney,' Sam said, breaking away from her as he got into his car.

'Sam,' Whitney pressed. She grabbed his arm but he shook free again. 'Jesus, I can't believe you! Have you no respect? We were married, Sam. For fifteen years! Doesn't that mean *anything*?'

'Evidently not,' he said. 'Or you wouldn't have fucked the lawn guy.'

He got in the car, fired up the engine and left Whitney standing on the sidewalk with that little gem to mull over as he drove on out of there.

Roxy made it to the front of Abby's apartment block and banged on every buzzer until one let her in. She skipped the lift, heading immediately for the stairs.

Abby's new apartment was on the third floor. Roxy bounded up the stairs, her heart beating with each footstep. She crashed through the double doors, out of the stairwell and into the hallway. She found Abby's place and banged on the door. When she got no answer, she tried the door handle. It turned.

Roxy stood by the open door.

'Abby?' she called? 'It's me, Rox. Are you in there?'

There was no answer.

She heard sounds from the living room. Sounded like voices. She pushed the door further open and was ambushed by a familiar stench. She made a face at the putrid odor and went to call out to Abby again, but her voice cracked.

Roxy swallowed hard, called again.

Nothing. She moved down the corridor, stopping dead at the sight of charred footprints burned in the wooden floorboards. A trail of blistered wallpaper on either side. Cheap art hanging crooked, their glass cracked and their frames warped as if by extreme heat.

'Shit," Roxy muttered under her breath. Her hand found the grigri bag, pinched it, and then rolled it between her fingers and thumb as she hurried forward, pushing the living room door open, and entered the room. There was no one there.

The sound was clearer now and she realized it wasn't voices. A record was spinning on the player, the needle bouncing on the one groove, the same lyric sounding over and over again. Even with one line, Roxy could tell it was that old record Lori used to play: Voodoo Child by Jimi Hendrix.

More charred footprints. She tracked their path, across the room and up to the back of the couch where they suddenly stopped. She looked down. The couch was in disarray.

Chunky cushions lying cockeyed and singed. One on the floor decorated with a charred footprint. Thrown pillows strewn about. Coffee table turned on its side. A partial handprint burned into the wooden frame. Another burned into a broken table leg lying nearby.

Roxy imagined Abby waking from a nap to find someone standing behind the couch, looking down at her. She had a good idea who that someone might have been, but stopped short of allowing the image to manifest in her thoughts.

She went to the record player, lifted the needle and set it back on the holder. The record stopped spinning. The room became quiet.

She heard a sound from the kitchen, turned sharply.

'Abby? That you?'

Roxy searched the room for a weapon of some kind, grabbed an old lamp with a metal base, removed the lampshade, and flipped it in her hand. Brandishing the thing like a bludgeon, she left the living room, heading back down the hallway to the apartment's kitchen, rolling the grigri bag, stopping only to push the door open.

'Abby, come on girl. You're scaring me—' a gasp leapt from Roxy's mouth snatching her words away prematurely.

Broken dishes everywhere, as if someone had made a game of hurling them at the cheap tile flooring. There was a sputtering sound to her right, kinda like water struggling to go down a blocked sink. When Roxy turned towards it, her expression fell, color draining from her face. It was Abby. Her friend stood against the wall, hands pinned to the noticeboard with two ice picks. A calendar hung open above her head. The pages were partially singed. A couple of dates were circled, the words BLACK WATER TRIP scrawled in the space in blue ink. Red blood soaked Abby's white night shirt, which appeared to have melted to her skin in random spots. The exposed skin covered in blisters and cooked flesh. A vertical stab-wound in her stomach large enough to stick a hand through.

An unexpected spasm and Abby was suddenly alive, if barely. The vertical wound belched forth a thick stream of blood.

Roxy's stomach did backflips.

Blood gurgled from Abby's mouth like thick milkshake, choking her as she tried to say something.

'Fuck,' Roxy managed.

She moved to help Abby, but the girl shook her head, more blood spewing from her mouth and from the wound in her stomach. Roxy noticed teeth marks all over her face and neck. It looked like an animal had savaged her.

'Jesus, girl. What do I do, what do I do?'

But Abby couldn't speak. Her voice was gone, a mere rasp with neither strength nor meaning. She was trying to say something but Roxy ignored her, prising the ice pick from Abby's left hand, the pain evident across her friend's face.

'I'm sorry,' Roxy cried, dropping the first pick to the floor then reaching for the other, starting to work on it.

She scanned the room for a phone, finding the cordless lying facedown on a nearby counter. Blood smeared across its back suggested that Abby had tried, in vain, to call for help.

The record player screeched into action again but this time it wasn't Hendrix. The distinct sound of a wailing harmonica filled the room.

Abby's eyes suddenly swelled, fixed upon something behind Roxy.

Roxy turned just in time.

The blade swirled by her, burrowing instead into the neck of Abby. A short gasp escaped Abby's mouth as more blood was spilled.

Roxy screamed, dropping immediately, losing the lamp base in the process. Kicking with her feet, she skittered along the kitchen floor. Dish shards skewered her weighty palms, but the pain paled in comparison to what Abby's eyes conveyed.

The killer pulled the knife from Abby, stared down at Roxy.

Abby's body slumped to the floor, her dead weight pulling the second ice pick all the way out. The killer turned, kicked Abby's still body once, twice. There was no movement. Satisfied, the killer turned back to Roxy.

The face was hidden beneath Geordi's burlap mask, but the hair poking out from under it and the body standing there with the cane knife was decidedly female... and all too familiar to Roxy. Ethereal vapours cackled around her and a living swarm of red scribble moved about the faceless burlap as the woman cricked her head to the side. She reached up, pulled the mask off, and tossed it to the floor just as a word had begun to materialize from the scribble. Something that started with the letter "B."

'L-Lori?' Roxy managed even though it made absolutely no sense to her.

But it was Lori alright. That face, that smile – both were warped into a ghoulish caricature by a veil of supernatural heat. Her long beaded hair and wide eyes that had gone completely white. Those clothes. The fucking bangles on her wrist, jingling like bells.

'Jesus fuck,' Roxy yelled, 'It was *you* the whole time?!'

The other girl smiled, nodded. Her teeth were bloodied like she'd been sucking the very blood from Abby's mutilated body.

'But why?!'

'Why not?' The voice that fell from Lori's mouth wasn't Lori's at all. It was a male voice and again very familiar.

Roxy's blood froze in her very veins.

'D-Danny?'

'Hello, baby,' he said. 'Been a while.'

FORTY ONE

Sam entered the corridor and quickly found the door to Abby's apartment. He was just about to knock when he heard a scream. He drew his gun and pushed through the door.

The front door was closest to the kitchen so that's where he went first, taking mental notes of the layout along the way. Singed footprints. Blistered wallpaper. Crocked wall art peeking out from behind broken glass. Frames warped by extreme heat.

What the hell had happened here?

Sam shoved the kitchen door open and saw Abby's body. She lay on the floor below the noticeboard, arms outstretched, eyes wide open, blood everywhere. The look on her face sent chills down his spine.

Geordi's hollow burlap dome was lying on its side a few feet away, its featureless face adorned with red scribble and glyphs. A cordless phone stained with blood lay facedown on the counter.

Another scream, this time coming from the bedroom.

Sam ran down the hall, through the living room, towards the bedroom door on the other side.

He pushed open the bedroom door, finding Roxy standing over a bleeding Lori. She held a knife aloft – a cane knife – ready to attack. Lori's arms were raised to protect herself. Big brown eyes radiated sheer terror.

Sam felt his heart stop dead in his chest, but his trigger finger kept on working. He fired once, hitting Roxy, the young stripper losing grip on the cane knife and falling to the floor.

Still keeping his gun trained on the felled girl, Sam entered the room. He reached his foot to the knife on the floor, gently moving it away from Roxy's reach.

'Oh God!' wailed Lori. 'Oh God oh God oh God…'

'Just try to relax,' Sam said, sheathing his gun and stooping to check her wound. It looked to be a flesh wound but she was still bleeding fairly 'You need to put pressure on that,' he said. Took out his handkerchief and showed Lori how. 'Keep your hands pressed against the hanky. I'm going to call for an ambulance.'

His heart was like a lead weight sinking into his gut, now. The image of Roxy falling was playing out in his head over and over again.

Lori looked terrified, her face drained of color.

Sam touched his hand to her cheek. 'You're going to be okay,' he said. 'Now, I need to go grab the phone but I'll be right back.'

Sam made his way to the kitchen where he remembered seeing the cordless. His mind was a mess, his body kicking into sheriff mode to cope.

The Sawyer girl was alive? And Roxy? Jesus, she'd been part of this thing all along. That's what the old woman had meant when she'd told Bonaparte that it wasn't the cowboy. She must have known her granddaughter was still alive and wanted to protect the girl.

It was all clicking into place, now. The whole damn thing was making some fucked up kind of sense to Sam.

He reckoned Roxy had gone AWOL once he'd rang her at the club. By her own twisted psychopath logic, Roxy had decided she needed to finish what was started and hurried to Abby's place before Sam closed in on her. But her unmasking was a complete shock to the sheriff. He'd acted on instinct alone: it broke his heart to have to fire on a girl he could have just as easily fallen in love with.

His hands were shaking as he lifted the phone. He averted his eyes from Abby's body rather than see the terrified look on her face again. He pressed for a dial tone, punched in 911 and raised the receiver to his ear. An operator answered and Sam was just about to speak when he caught whiff of an odor so rotten that it burned his senses.

There was a sudden heat against his back.

FORTY TWO

Roxy's eyes flicked open, the world slowly coming into view again. A putrid stench lingered in the air. She coughed, a spatter of blood peppering the bedroom carpet. She could feel her heart beating, its dumpa-dumpa-dumpa rhythm kickstarting her senses. She went to move, felt a sharp pain eating into her upper back, and winced. She slowly rose up to her knees.

Her eyes searched the bedroom.

Lori… *Danny…* was gone.

So was the cane knife.

She had vague memories of seeing Sheriff Taylor. Of him aiming his gun and then…

And then it hit her.

Oh God, no!

Roxy fought against the waves of nausea and dizziness, rising to her feet. She struggled towards the door then made her way from room to room.

She found Lori in the kitchen, standing behind Sam Taylor who was on his knees shaking as if from a sustained electric shock as Lori held him there with a hand clasped over his mouth. Abby's body was on the floor and it looked like the sheriff would be joining her very soon.

'Lori, stop!' Roxy shouted.

Lori turned and stared in her direction. Her eyes had gone white again, her blade still on Sam's throat. The sheriff's eyes found Roxy's. He looked confused and scared and sorry all at once. Smoke rose from his shoulders and from the top of his head as the Devil Vapor burned through his clothing,

cooked his flesh, and singed his hair.

'Not Lori. You know that,' Danny replied, his voice strong and natural through Lori's lips.

But then he smiled. It wasn't his smile so Roxy seized upon that, 'I know there's still something of you in there,' she said, still addressing her friend and not Danny. 'Please, Lori. I need you to come back. Please…'

But the other girl's head shook.

'The lights may be on,' Danny said. 'But there ain't nobody but me home.' And with that, the blade drew across Sam Taylor' throat.

Lori's hands released him and Sam looked to Roxy as he swayed back and forth, clutching at his throat, his eyes swollen in stark realization of his pending death, the skin around his mouth all charred and blistered.

She stared back, her lips shaping, 'I'm sorry,' as he fell forward and faceplanted on the cheap tile, tendrils of smoke marking his slow descent.

Blood dripped from the cane knife in Lori's

hands and Roxy found herself wondering just how much life could be stolen by the one blade.

She backed into the hallway, sheer terror numbing the pain of the gunshot wound in her shoulder. She made for the bedroom, slamming the door behind her then locking it, and sliding down onto the floor.

Her hands were soaked in sweat. She wiped them on the leather of her skirt then ran them through her hair. She squeezed her eyes shut, hoping that her heart would stop thumping, that the blood would flow quicker from the wound in her shoulder and she could pass away peacefully.

There was a knock. She knew it was Danny.

'Go away!' she protested. Tears filled her eyes and she started to sob. 'Go away go away go away!'

Her hands beat uselessly against the door.

A rat-a-tat-tat knock came in response, then Danny's voice, playacting as Lori, 'But I'm your friend, Roxy. Why won't you let me in?' Laughter, then hammering accompanied by, 'Open up the door, bitch, or I'm going to hack it down then hack *you* down!'

Roxy searched the bedroom for some way of escape but there was nothing. The only window was covered with security bars. Her eyes fell upon a bag of disposable razors next to a neatly folded towel on the dresser. She could take one out, use it to speed her own blood loss. End it all here and now.

Roxy felt for the grigri bag, pinched it between her fingers and rolled. In her mind she could see Christie Keller standing by that lake, surrounded by the town's women folk. She didn't even know if it was Christie Keller's hair at all in there. Hell, maybe it was the old man's hair or his wife's. But one thing was sure: it gave Roxy the extra kick she needed. Witch or no witch, Christie Keller was a girl who knew something about mad folks wanting to kill her for no reason.

'Come on, you bitch! Open up and get your dues!'

The old Roxy rose up from within. The part of her who wanted to fight this bastard with every last ounce of strength and blood she still had left. Hell, he'd killed Abby, Lori…

…*He'd killed Sam.*

More banging on the door.

Roxy couldn't stand it anymore.

She stood to her feet, felt around her waist for the studded belt attached to her skirt. She removed the belt, looped it around her fist. She lifted the grigri bag to her lips, kissed it for good measure. Ol' Gramps had protected her so far. That's why the Devil Vapor hadn't affected her like it had that night at the Stogies, like it had with Sam and Abby tonight. She knew that now.

As the hammering continued, Roxy flicked the lock then pulled the door open, aiming the hand wrapped in studded leather towards her bemused assailant.

Roxy heard a crack as Lori's jawbone snapped under the impact. But she didn't stop, instead stepping forward, pushing against Lori's body and throwing another punch. Then another. She was screaming now. Hammering her way out into the middle of the living room, pushing her attacker backward.

There was a half-assed attempt at swinging the knife, but Roxy dodged it, the blade swinging over her head. Roxy threw another punch at Lori's already pummelled face. The knife fell to the floor, Lori's body following. But Roxy didn't stop, instead grabbing the long handle of the knife, straddling her fallen assailant, raising the blade with both hands before bringing it down ONCE, TWICE, THREE TIMES. The Devil Vapor flickered in and out with each blow and then dissipated into the ether. A sunburst of charred floorboards surrounded them.

Roxy raised the knife once more...

A soft voice called out in protest. Brown eyes pleaded.

Roxy snapped out of her trance, dropped the blade.

'Lori?' she called.

'R-Rox...'

'Shhhh, don't speak, girl,' Roxy said.

Tears broke across her friend's face. 'I'm sorry, Rox,' she whimpered. 'I really am. Nanna was right. Should never have done that magic on Abby. Danny.... he got inside me and I couldn't stop him. I could see... f-feel every... but couldn't stop...'

Lori's eyes rolled back into her head.

'Lori?!' Roxy cried. 'Lori, look at me!'

But it was no use. Lori was gone.

Roxy pulled herself to her feet. She looked at her hands. They were covered in blood. Lori's blood. She wiped them on her skirt, stepped over Lori's body and returned to the kitchen.

Sam's body lay sprawled on the floor right next to Abby.

A police siren whirred in the distance. The sound drew closer. After all the hammering and screaming and shooting someone had finally called the cops. And when they got here, they'd find sole survivor Roxy with three bodies, packing a bullet from a registered police firearm. Her prints were everywhere. All over the apartment, the knife. They'd throw the book at her and then some. Death penalty for sure.

Roxy bent down to rustle Sam's hair. The back of his head was badly burned. The white collar of his shirt ran red with blood. His tie was loosened, the knot pulled way too tight and small. He'd removed his wedding ring, finally, and Roxy figured that meant he'd had his day in court.

Roxy pressed two fingers against her lips and then rested them on Sam Taylor's cheek. His skin was lifeless, cold and clammy. Roxy closed her eyes, leaned in to his ear and whispered something that he wouldn't hear.

The sirens were getting closer. But Roxy did one more thing before leaving. She went into the living room and fired up the old record player, moving the needle to the start of the seven inch.

She half expected to hear the haunting wail of a harmonica again but, instead, the opening bars to Voodoo Child played.

EPILOGUE

The Motel room was exactly what Roxy expected. Four walls with no life and little identity, perfect for a girl on the run.

She lay on the single bed watching the portable television, hooked into the wall right opposite. Her picture was on the screen, the local newsreader describing her as 'a serial killer on the loose. Likely to be armed and certainly dangerous.'

Roxy switched the TV off, got up. She guessed it was time to go. Pack up and hit the road again, continue this endless and mindless routine she'd come to know so well.

The door to the bathroom was open; its light beaming despite the rays of sun poking through the room's drawn blinds. Roxy stepped inside and looked in the mirror. The face that looked back was notably different from the one on the television. She'd cut her hair short, dyed it brown. Her make-up was lighter and she wore glasses. She looked younger, more innocent. A loose basketball sweatshirt hung around an even slimmer frame than normal.

Jesus, she thought. *I look like Abby.*

A knock came to the door and Roxy automatically froze.

Roxy reached almost instinctually for the grigri bag around her neck.

Still there.

More knocking, followed by a voice, announcing itself as the maid.

Roxy sighed, went to the door and opened it

on the chain.

It was an older Mexican woman. Her name tag said 'Leandra'. She wore deep red lipstick and dark green eye shadow. Her hair was dark and packed tighter curls than Roxy could even dream of.

The maid peeked through the slim gap and asked, 'Will you be staying another night, Miss?'

A voice in Roxy's head said, 'Invite her in. Then kill her,' but Roxy ignored it instead telling the maid that she would be leaving soon and asking if she would mind calling back later.

The maid smiled in a carefree way and then moved onto the next room.

Roxy closed the door.

'A razor oughta do it,' the voice in her head suggested.

'Would you shut the fuck up?' Roxy replied.

'Make me,' the voice coaxed.

'Alright, I will,' Roxy countered.

She moved back to the bathroom, opened the cabinet and retrieved a small bottle of pills. Anti-psychotic drugs. Roxy opened the lid and popped two. She replaced the bottle, went to the sink. She leaned to the cold tap, ran some water through her mouth and swallowed the pills. She turned the tap off and looked once more in the mirror.

'Fuck you, Danny,' she said.

She didn't know exactly when he'd left Lori's body and entered her own but figured it was some time during their last struggle. And he'd been working on Roxy just liked he'd no doubt worked on Lori: slowly poisoning her mind;

trying to manipulate her the way men like him manipulated people all their lives. But Danny wouldn't get the better of a girl like Roxy Blue. She had always been a hard-nosed bitch and this whole ordeal had made her even tougher. In fact, Danny would never hurt another man, woman or child while Roxy was living; regardless of how many pills it took to keep his damn trap shut.

'Can't keep hiding me,' she heard him say now, as his voice faded. 'You'll slip up and I'll slip in. Just you watch. No escape, right? Just you...'

'Yeah, yeah,' Roxy whispered feeling once more for the grigri bag. 'Yeah fucking yeah.'

ABOUT THE AUTHORS

WAYNE SIMMONS

Belfast born, Wayne Simmons, loitered with intent around the genre circuit for some years. He penned reviews and interviews for several online zines before publication of his debut novel, Drop Dead Gorgeous, in 2008.

Wayne's work has since been published in the UK, Austria, Germany, Spain, Turkey and North America. His bestselling zombie novel, Flu, was serialised by Sirius XM's Book Radio.

He's a regular contributor to Skin Deep Tattoo Magazine and Power Play as well as the PR/Marketing chief for Infected Books. In 2013 and 2014, Wayne co-produced the popular Scardiff Horror Expo.

Wayne currently lives in Wales with his ghoulfiend and a Jack Russel terrier called Dita. Look out for him at various genre, music and tattoo events.

www.waynesimmons.org
facebook.com/wayne.simmons.1048
@HorrorHoo

ABOUT THE AUTHORS

ANDRE DUZA

Andre Duza is an actor, screenwriter, and a leading member of the Bizarro movement in contemporary literary fiction. His novels include WZMB, King Dollar, Technicolor Terrorists, Necro Sex Machine, Jesus Freaks, Dead Bitch Army, and the graphic novel, Hollow-Eyed Mary. He is the co-author of Son of a Bitch co-written with Wrath James White, and Outer Light, a graphic novel sequel to a Hugo Award Winning episode of Star Trek: The Next Generation that was penned by television writer/producer Morgan Gendel.

He has also contributed to such collections and anthologies as Book of Lists: Horror alongside the likes of Stephen King, Edgar Wright and Eli Roth.

www.houseofduza.com
facebook.com/andreduza

If you are the original purchaser of this book, or if you received this book as a gift, you can download a complementary eBook version by visiting:

www.infectedbooks.co.uk/ebooks

and completing the necessary information (terms and conditions apply).

Or take a Shelfie!

A **free** eBook edition is available with the purchase of this print book.

CLEARLY PRINT YOUR NAME ABOVE IN UPPER CASE

Instructions to claim your free eBook edition:
1. Download the BitLit app for Android or iOS
2. Write your name in **UPPER CASE** on the line
3. Use the BitLit app to submit a photo
4. Download your eBook to any device

Lightning Source UK Ltd.
Milton Keynes UK
UKOW02f0216060416

271661UK00002B/9/P